GOTHIC NOVELS

GOTHIC NOVELS

Advisory Editor:
Dr. Sir Devendra P. Varma

THE
LIBERTINE

Volume 3

CHARLOTTE DACRE

("ROSA MATILDA")

New Foreword by John Garrett

New Introduction by Devendra P. Varma

ARNO PRESS

A New York Times Company

New York—1974

Reprint Edition 1974 by Arno Press Inc.

Special Contents Copyright © 1974
   by Devendra P. Varma

Reprinted from a copy in
   The University of Illinois Library

GOTHIC NOVELS II
ISBN for complete set: 0-405-06011-4
See last pages of this volume for titles.

Manufactured in the United States of America

————•————

Library of Congress Cataloging in Publication Data

Dacre, Charlotte, b. 1782.
   The libertine.

   (Gothic novels II)
   Reprint of the 1807 ed. printed for T. Cadell and W.
Davies, London.
   I. Title. II. Series.
PZ3.D123Li4   [PR4525.D119]   823'.7   73-22761
ISBN 0-405-06012-2

THE

LIBERTINE,

BY

CHARLOTTE DACRE,

BETTER KNOWN AS

ROSA MATILDA.

AUTHOR OF

Hours of Solitude, Nun of St. Omer's, Zofloya, &c.

IN FOUR VOLUMES.

VOL. III.

If one by one you wedded all the world,
Or from the all that are, took something good
To make a perfect woman; she you kill'd
Would be unparallel'd.

SHAKESPEARE.

.... Are not these strange self delusions, and yet attested by common experience?　　　　SOUTH.

LONDON:

PRINTED FOR T. CADELL AND W. DAVIES, STRAND.

1807.

LIBERTINE.

CHAP. XVIII.

Time crept on, and all hope of discovering their child faded gradually and sorrowfully from the minds of the parents. Felix had attained his tenth year, and on him alone rested now their fond expectations. But the mind of the mother would often revert with a sigh of bitter regret to the probable fate of her beloved Agnes, who would now have been for her so sweet a companion, and filled up with delight many moments that were necessarily devoted to solitude; for Felix was more the companion of his

father than her, and though a lovely
and engaging youth, he needed that ur-
banity, softness, and docility of manner
which fondly she imagined in the gentle
creature she had lost. The idol of his
father, it was not unfrequently that she
beheld insufficient her mild and rational
controul to restrain the impetuosity of
his manners, the wildness, and often
serious impropriety of his conduct. But
Angelo, who contended that all this was
but the ardour and spirit of youth, and
that it would yield to the soberer influence of judgment and increase of years,
loved not that she should check the boy;
for in the fulness of a proud self-love he
would remember, that his son resembled
what he himself had been at his age.

Thus by the mismanagement, and of-
tentimes imprudent interference of Angelo in his presence, many errors were

suffered to take deep and fatal root in
the heart of Felix, which the anxious
vigilance and salutary reproofs of his
mother might have timely extirpated,
but would at all events have rendered of
little influence in his future general character. Still she entertained hopes that
unremitting perseverance on her side,
and the ultimate prevalence of increasing
reason over early folly, on his, would
correct the imperfections of his present
disposition, and render him all that her
anxious love desired to behold him as a
man.

The hopes of Gabrielle were however
doomed to be frustrated, for the conduct
of Felix, his inattention to her counsels,
and disobedience of her commands, ori-
ginated in a source deeper far than any
of which she was aware ; for while she
considered as the wandering of the head

merely, the errors of her child, they sprang from a heart corrupted and contaminated by the baneful influence of surrounding circumstance.

In the domestic establishment of Angelo, was a female named Milborough ; she had been originally hired to attend exclusively upon the infant Felix, and to keep a guard over him, excepting when under the eyes of his parents. As Felix grew older however, and required no longer the vigilant care of a nurse, Gabrielle conceiving a regard for the woman on account of the attention she considered her to have bestowed upon her charge, retained her still in the family to officiate as a personal attendant upon herself. Nothing could be more gentle, modest, and unassuming than the general conduct of Milborough, nothing more treacherous, base, and diabolical

than her heart : nothing could equal
the propriety of her deportment but the
depravity of her principles ; nor any thing
the conciliating anxiety she evinced to
obey the smallest of Gabrielle's desires,
but the secret, malign, and unprovoked
hatred which she bore her.

Possessed of a profligate intriguing spirit, she veiled it with the profoundest art,
and under the guise of an inoffensive pla-
cidity, concealed a mercenary and deceitful soul ; all she said, and all she did,
bore the stamp of candour and disin-
terestedness ; her countenance was never
ruffled by impatience at reproof, she
heard all with submission, but felt with
rancour, and revenged with bitterness.

Soon after her introduction to the family, by an unfortunate accident, but
one too easy of occurrence in a situation

not strictly conformable to propriety and
virtue, this woman had discovered that
marriage was not the tie which bound in
a union apparently so indissoluble those
persons who gave her bread; and far
from closing her eyes and ears, as duty
dictated to a menial like herself, against
a secret thus betrayed, she spared no
opportunity of endeavouring to confirm,
by prying curiosity, and unobserved remark, the truth of what at first had been
but vaguely made known to her. She
soon gained, or conceived that she did,
proof sufficient to convince her. From
that moment, those bad principles with
which her soul was imbued were called
into action ; she no longer bore towards
Gabrielle the smallest respect, viewing
her no more in the light of a superior,
though she still appeared to do so ; for
it is an invariable maxim with vulgar
minds, when they discover aught amiss

in those above them, immediately to
place themselves upon a level with them,
to consider all inequality at an end, and
establish their own claims to distinction,
merely upon a comparative view with
their errors. Thus was it with Milborough, who not taking into her narrow
conception the superior birth, merits,
or high qualities of Gabrielle, saw simply an unjust difference in their present
stations, and imagined when she beheld
her unpolished figure in the glass, that
her title to rank and opulence was in no
way inferior to that of her mistress.
This ignorant and presumptuous idea
laid the foundation of a train of evils at
once mighty and incalculable.

The commands of Gabrielle, now that
she beheld her in a light so humiliated,
no more enforced obedience from her as
a duty; consequently she obeyed reluc-

tantly, for they galled and offended her; and she made herself amends for her condescension by every means in her power. Being from her situation (which her interest would not permit her to resign) so placed as to be necessarily subordinate to Gabrielle, she from first thinking herself degraded by obeying her, ultimately hated her who commanded; yet this low born upstart presumed to consider *Gabrielle* a mark for envy, therefore for hatred; and in proportion as her high and superior virtues manifested themselves, supported by a steady dignity, the result of conscious nobility of mind, as well as birth, the hatred of this reptile increased with every foul aggravation which low minded malice could conceive, venting itself in secret, unsuspected, but dreadful mischief.

Though at the period of her entering
the service of Angelo, Felix tenderly
loved his mother, yet Milborough, from
being constantly with him, acquired a
sort of *second love* in his heart, which
soon usurped the place of the first,—an
undue and irrational influence on his
mind likewise, such as vulgar cunning
suggests, may be easiest obtained over
youth and inexperience. It was by
yielding ever to his follies and caprices,
acquiescing with a smile in his wildest sallies, by indiscriminate indulgence, improper temptations to disobey
the anxious or rational injunctions of
his mother; flattery, inducing him to
commit faults for the purpose of raising
her consequence in his eyes by conceal-
ing them, and gaining his confidence
and affection through the channel of a
perverted gratitude.

Felix grew fond of his nurse; his boyish mind preferred her society to that
of his mother, who content to see him
happy, was never displeased at his anxiety to return to Milborough after being
a short time absent from her; and from
being merely induced to think from
that circumstance that she treated the
boy with kindness, continually bestowed
on her marks of her gratitude and satisfaction; thus unconsciously cherishing
a snake, who was stinging her in the tenderest point. When Felix, still very young,
had committed one day a slight error for
which Gabrielle considered it necessary
to reprove him, but did it in the mild-
est and most gentle manner, Felix burst
into tears, and sought his flattering nurse,
who perceiving her pretended favourite
weeping bitterly, took him immediately
in her arms, and inquired the cause of
his distress. Felix, certain of being pi-

tied and soothed, informed her, while his tears redoubled; when giving vent to her secret malice, Milborough exclaimed,

" Indeed !—but *she* has no right to be angry with you, Felix."

"Oh yes," cried the boy, instantly checking his tears, and looking up in her face, struck as it appeared by so base an insinuation.—" Certainly my mother has a right to be angry with me."

" Indeed she has not, Felix," answered Milborough, with a lip of contempt, " your father has a right, but she is *nobody.*"

" Nobody! Milborough," cried Felix, looking at her indignantly;—" my mo-

ther nobody? I do not understand you,"
and, instinctively as it were, he withdrew
her arm from round his neck.

" Why, Felix, you are too young to
understand indeed, so let us say no more
about it."

But the curiosity of youth is not so
easily appeased ; this the artful Milborough reckoned on, and when a few minutes after Felix required an explanation of what she had meant by saying
his mother was "nobody," her eyes
sparkled with the exultation of malice,
and her base heart rejoiced at the
thought of the revenge she was taking
upon the excellence, and imagined happiness of Gabrielle, which she died to
frustrate.

" Why then," with pretended hesitation she replied—"I will tell you,—but first promise me never to mention it to any one, but above all, not to your mother."

"Oh, but my mother says I must never have any secrets from her," answered Felix.

"Pho, nonsense," returned Milborough, putting her arm round him again, which action, his curiosity now on the stretch, he did not again repulse.—" Now listen."

The little Felix opened his ears to drink in the base pernicious communications of the abandoned Milborough ; and she availing herself of the deep attention with which he listened, made as clear as she possibly could to his childish capacity, that there was a certain cere-mony called marriage, which if not duly and regularly performed between two persons deciding to live together, the female lost all consequence in society, and was regarded as an unfit companion for other females, honourably married ; hat the children, likewise, were never considered by the world as entitled to any distinction, but on the contrary ; and that therefore they were not obliged to honour or obey a mother whom no one honoured or esteemed, and who had so little considered in her conduct their future welfare or estimation in society. "Thus, Felix, you perceive I was right," she concluded, "in saying that your mother was nobody."

Felix was silent, his mind was confused, he felt something like painful conviction, and this conversation made a deep impression. Above all, he remembered a sensation of uneasiness which he had ex-

perienced at that part of Milborough's
discourse wherein she had made an observation respecting the opinion which the
world entertained of children situated as
he now understood himself to be.

A frequent recurrence to that most
infamous insinuation produced a baleful
effect upon his character : he endeavoured, child as he was, to divest himself of
all pride, conceiving from what Milborough had said, he had no right to possess any, and in so doing unfortunately
divested himself of *that* pride which is
the foundation of every virtue, the pride
of principle. As he grew older, the de-
structive effect of this idea produced
daily more lamentable consequences.
He lost all self respect, all solicitude for
proper conduct; he said to himself, "However good, honourable, or virtuous I may
be, no one will look at me, or think me

worthy notice." Thus is it but too true,
that however injurious may be an excess
of pride, to be wholly devoid of it is to be
devoid of every virtue ; for when we
despise ourselves, we are indifferent to
the approbation of others, to the noble
distinction of superior worth, and all that
gives consideration to the man.

Unhappily for Gabrielle, she knew
not the corruption that had been engen-
dered in the heart of her son ; she knew
not the dreadful sentiments that there
had taken root, or her anxious counsels,
her just and animated representation of
that wherein true virtue and dignity
consist, depending solely on the mind,
and on the heart, towering singly, and unaided, neither to be raised or depreciated
by surrounding circumstances, but making in itself the nobility of the indivi-
dual ; had she but been aware, she might

have destroyed the evil in its germ, and
applied the remedy ere it had proved in
vain.

Her who had been the nurse of his
childhood, as Felix advanced to maturer
years became the friend, the adviser of
his youth, the faithful depositary, and
often partaker of his secret follies and
intentions; he now understood perfectly, from the frequent questions he had
proposed to Milborough, and which she
ever answered with unwearied readiness;
from combining in his naturally intelli-
gent mind such ideas as presented
themselves, from observation, or an in-
quisitiveness of spirit, all which at first
he had found it difficult to comprehend.
From the joint operation of these circumstances his respect for his mother
gradually decreased; with it decreased
his love likewise, and involved with the

dereliction the finer and better qualities
of his soul ; for filial love and respect
cannot causelessly quit the young mind
without depriving it of some of its best
and brightest virtues.

The abandoned Milborough rejoiced
in the train of mischief she was secretly
laying, which in time she hoped to see
explode, causing dreadful and unspeak-
able havoc. The boyish partiality of
Felix for her increased rather than diminished with his years—she was so gentle,
so yielding, so ever ready to acquiesce in
all his wishes however difficult to be at-
chieved; she appeared too so happy when
she could compass for him any point he
desired, so delighted to favour or oblige
him. Being frequently the companion
of his father, he would sometimes in the
plenitude of youthful exhiliration speak
of her in terms of highest praise. An-

gelo would listen with a smile; he was
not surprised at the fondness of a young
boy for the woman who had been a kind
nurse to him in his childhood, but he was
wholly incompetent to judge of the merits
of Milborough; she did not come within
his sphere, and he had scarcely ever bestowed on her a moment's attention. Induced at
length by the reiterated observations of
the youth in her favour, he one morning,
when she entered the room where he was
sitting with Gabrielle, raised mechani-
cally his eyes to her face.—He beheld
there an expression of modesty and in-
genuousness which pleased him, and sufficient attraction to obviate the charge
of ugliness, an attraction which, though
devoid of youth or beauty, boasted a
sort of charm independent of either.

Felix, who had remarked with pleasure that his father had noticed Milbo-

rough, seized the first opportunity of
their being alone to ask him if he did
not think Milborough handsome.

" Not particularly so," was the reply
of Angelo; " but since she has deported
herself so well towards you, tell her from
me, that whenever she chuses to marry,
I will give her a sufficient portion to en-
sure the good-will of her husband."

Felix, delighted at the idea of having
so pleasing a communication to make to
Milborough, and hoping that it would
infinitely raise his consequence with her,
hastened when he left his father to impart it to her. Scarce had Milborough
heard him to an end, ere an idea flashed across her mind which tinged her
cheek with the fire of exultation; she
beheld in the munificent promise of Angelo, not merely what it proposed, but

far more that it implied; disguising her
joy however, she with an apparent modesty and humility entreated Felix to
return her most grateful thanks to her
lord, but with an air of embarrassment
added, that she had no intention of ever
marrying.

That night, sleep was a stranger to
the eyes of Milborough; visions of aspiring hope floated before her; extravagant presumptuous calculations filled
her brain, and she wondered at her dul-
ness in having so long failed to see the
road which lay most open for her to opulence and grandeur, but above all, to
compass that destruction in which unceasingly she had longed to involve her
envied hated mistress. The casual notice of Angelo, and the intimation sent
her by him through Felix, formed the
basis of her present golden dreams.

Since he had deigned to listen to her
praises, and so far acquiesced in their
justice as to send her a special embassy
proving his disposition in her favour,
what might she not in reason expect?
Well she knew she could not appreciate
too highly the estimation in which she
was held by Felix. He possessed an
unlimited influence over his father, it
was only therefore to render him voluntarily or involuntarily, no matter which,
the medium of introducing her more
fully to the observation of Angelo, and
her most sanguine anticipations might
be easily fulfilled.

Pursuant to this idea, she redoubled
her attention towards the son, and threw
herself, as much as her department in the
family would allow, without suspicion,
in the way of the father; she endeavoured by every artifice compleatly to estrange

the affections of Felix from his mother,
and to court him from her society to her
own. For this purpose she filled her
apartment with entertainment for him,
drawing materials, with subjects more
amusing than instructive, from which
to copy, books, pernicious rather than
edifying, musical instruments and songs
that she accompanied him with, calculated from their tendency to corrupt the
heart and mislead the imagination. Milborough, who had not an indifferent
voice, one evening carelessly and with
a smile observed to Felix, after conclud-
ing a song, " Do you not think, Felix,
that my lord would like to hear some of
our songs ?"

" I am certain he would," answered
Felix eagerly, " but you would not sing
before my mother, Milborough."

"How simple you are," returned Milborough; "certainly not."

"Shall I ask my father then to come and hear you?" said Felix.

"Oh, not for the world," returned Milborough laughing, "I am certain I could not sing a note in the presence of my lord."

"Well, but if you did not see him?" cried Felix, smiling archly and looking at Milborough.

"Oh, perhaps I might then," answered the artful Milborough, catching his idea.

"To-morrow evening I will bring my father to hear you, as if by accident, and he shall remain in the next room to you."

" But he must not know," interposed Milborough, " that I have any knowledge of his being there."

" He shall not, indeed."

" Well, upon those terms," said Milborough with a musing air, but secretly rejoiced, and desiring to have the air of submitting to an arrangement of which she had been the first instigator, " upon those terms I think I have no objection."

" It is decided," cried Felix : " now let us have another song; and then I must leave you."

The next evening Felix proposed to his father to be an unseen auditor of Milborough's singing. Angelo, who had not the least anxiety to hear such vulgar

harmony as he conceived hers must be,
at first directly refused, but yielding to
the entreaty of his son, he at length consented, and promised, laughing, that he
would accompany him to the room ad-
joining hers for that purpose, at the time
mutually agreed on. When the hour
arrived, Angelo had forgotten his promise, but at the vexed remonstrance of
the impetuous youth, he yielded acquiescence, and followed him to the appointed spot. A small glass window fixed in
the door which separated the two rooms,
was usually covered with a curtain, but
the scheming Milborough, whose plan
was artfully laid, had drawn this curtain the least degree possible aside, yet
sufficiently, while it appeared the work
of accident, to give an insight into the
chamber. There accurately drest, that
is modestly, though to the highest advantage, she awaited the moment when by a

little signal previously agreed on between
her and Felix, she should be informed of
their entrance, and know when to begin
her song. No sooner had she received from
the unthinking boy the necessary hint,
than she commenced by carelessly humming an air, not without taste, which at
intervals she interrupted, as more intent
upon her employment, which was embroid-
ering flowers in a frame ; then gradually she entered on the song of the air she
had been humming. The subject was
simply interesting and artfully chosen.
It related to the concealed love of a maid
in lowly station for a lord of high rank,
and it painted her secret anguish in
mournful expression, and melancholy
tone, to which she managed to give peculiar effect, and concluded with the
death of the maid from her hopeless passion, in consequence of the marriage of her
lover with another.

While she sang, so apparently unconscious that any human being was nigh,
Angelo, whose expectations she had completely surpassed, for he had attributed
the praises of Felix merely to his want
of taste in the science, found himself first
involuntarily drawn towards the artfully
contrived aperture, better to catch the
notes of her voice, and next rivetted there,
by the well arranged figure and pleasing countenance which displayed itself
to his view.   He continued gazing near
a minute after the song was ended, and
was only roused from his intentness by
the gentle voice of Felix, who pulling
him by the arm, in the spirit of boyish
mischief whispered, " Let us break suddenly in upon Milborough, my lord,
and tell her we have heard her song,—
she will look so frightened and confused !"

" No, no, Felix," replied Angelo,
laughing, " what folly!"

" Oh, to oblige me, my lord—to oblige
me, my dear father ; do not refuse, I en-
treat you," said Felix ;. and dragging his
father forward, half reluctant, half careless, he with his foot burst open the door
which led into her room, and both stood
suddenly before her, Felix laughing im-
moderately at her confusion and alarm,
so well affected as to deceive even himself. But since Angelo had for the first
time entered her apartment. she was desirous to avail herself of the auspicious
moment. On their sudden entrance the
frame had fallen from her hand, she
started up, and appeared in the greatest
perturbation; now she trembled violently,
seeming unable to sustain herself, attempted to catch at a chair for support, and
failing, staggered and fell to the ground.

Angelo, somewhat flushed with wine, had given inconsiderately into the frolic of his son; but now seriously sorry for the terror he had occasioned a weak and timid female, he instinctively attempted to raise her from the ground, in which Felix, no longer gay and laughing, most earnestly assisted. At length Milborough appeared to recover, she was raised from the ground, but seeming suddenly to perceive that it was the hand of Angelo which held hers, to assist her, she swiftly withdrew it with a slight exclamation of alarm, and glanced on him a look, in which love struggling with apprehension, and pleasure with trembling timidity, were artfully contrasted. Angelo observed the expressive look; though past his youthful day, his natural character remained unchanged, at least in principle; ever open in a degree to the blandishments of women, he had not yet learnt to contemn them, and his vanity was still susceptible of being flattered by their admiration, as his heart to be influenced by their charms.

Thus Milborough, whose look had penetrated immediately to his self-love, began to wear additional attractions in his eyes; he now fancied there was meaning in the expression of her song, and while vanity faintly whispered that she dared to entertain an affection for him, self-love extenuated her presumption, and bade him pity, rather than despise her.

Honour and propriety would have dictated to Angelo at this imagined discovery, an unvarying countenance, excepting of increased coolness, and a speedy departure from her chamber, which if not expressive of his disgust, must have convinced her at least of the total impossibility of his supposing that

such a look directed to *him,* could contain the slightest meaning. But no, true
to the latent principles of his nature, of a
character that wanted energy, firmness,
and decision, that was ever acted on by
the influence of circumstance, or the moment, and was devoid of the dignified
fortitude which can resist adventitious
temptation, he suffered *more* softness to
be visible in his looks, more interest in
the tone of his voice, more tenderness in
the assistance he gave ; but all this was
urged by *pity,* and by the delicacy which
a woman commands from a man, who dis-
covers that she unhappily cherishes an
imprudent passion for him. Instead of
hastening from her room, as soon as possible, his stay was prolonged ; nor did he
quit her till he beheld her perfectly
recovered, and then with the hope, ex-
pressed in the gentlest accents, that by
the following day she would suffer no ill

effects from the alarm she had experienced.
Milborough seeming overpowered with
confusion, scarcely lifted her eyes from
the ground; and when Angelo rose for
the purpose of departing, she arose likewise, for he had compelled her to sit in
his presence, and seemed incapable, from
a sense of the honour conferred upon
her, of returning her faltering acknow-
ledgments for such condescension.

CHAPTER XIX.

———————

Who would not have believed, after so long a period of constancy and perseverance in the right path, that the follies of Angelo were for ever at an end ? Far otherwise ; the errors of the libertine are too frequently so imbued with the character, as to be invincible to the operation of time, experience, conscience, or reason, and to end but with the life of the wretched being they tyrannize over.

And on what had depended hitherto the virtue of Angelo? on what the peace

of the unhappy Gabrielle ? On accident
alone ; no meteor presenting itself to his
eyes, no attraction offering, he walked
directly forward, nothing occurring to
lead him astray ; he sought not temptation, if it sought not him, but if it did
he became its slave. Ill fated Gabrielle,
rejoice in the slender portion of happiness thou hast experienced, dream it o'er
in imagination, for never more shalt thou
experience its reality.

Novelty, in the form of Milborough,
presented itself to Angelo, and he was
incapable of resisting the attraction: it
is not *age* that checks the career of folly
in the libertine—no, his follies then become *vices*, they degenerate into depravity ; his feelings become vitiated, and
he possesses no longer that choice delica-
cacy of taste attendant on the pride of
youth. Thus, from having been in an

unguarded moment, by the influence of
an idle boy, induced to pay a slight
share of attention to a presumptuous
menial, he found himself involuntarily
interested, drawn frequently upon various pretexts to her apartment, and each
time of seeing her, that she occupied,
when out of her presence, an increased
portion of his thoughts. Her artful
demeanour tended greatly to strengthen
those at first vague impressions; in it he
saw, or fancied that he saw, a deep
concealed love struggling with the profoundest respect, and most invincible
timidity. If he entered suddenly, she
started, blushed, and trembled, forgot
her employment, hesitated, and knew
not whether to stand or sit. If she
chanced to meet him, which she likewise
endeavoured to do as frequently as possible, she stood still, seeming undecided
from confusion whether to pass him, or

turn back. Angelo was convinced by these
appearances, and while he compassion-
ated an unhappy love, he involuntarily
thought with tenderness of her who loved.

Mean time the conduct of Milborough towards Gabrielle was widely
different from the respect she evinced
for Angelo, and from what it had
formerly been to herself; it was such
precisely as a vulgar mind, impudently
elate in anticipated good fortune, must
manifest to one, whose high superiority
it had presumed to envy. Gabrielle,
mild as she was, became incensed at this
change in the manners of a domestic,
who had so much reason to persevere in
a proper line of conduct, and she taxed
her with her presumption in terms, for
her, unusually severe. At her just reproof,
the countenance of Milborough wore an
audacious expression, between a sneer

and a smile of triumph, and she deigned
not to utter a sentence in mitigation of
her faults.

It was the aim of this intriguing woman to bring as early as possible her
plans to bear ; she desired to provoke
Gabrielle to dismiss her from her service,
and while, to induce this result, she sought
by the most unqualified insolence and
offensive demeanour to try her patience
beyond endurance, she caused Felix to
represent to his father that she felt
such symptoms of indisposition, as
announced premature decay; at the
same time artfully intimating to the
youth that she wished her communications to be kept secret from all but himself, lest Gabrielle, who had become less
kind to her than formerly, should insist
on her removal ; and then, with false
tears, lamenting death only as it would

deprive her of the happiness of seeing her dear Felix a man.

This was sufficient to hasten Felix, who for this worthless being possessed an affection far greater than for his amiable mother, to disclose to his father her most important secret. Angelo, with a momentary flutter at his heart, saw it was for him she pined—he felt interested ; and half determined in his mind, that if Gabrielle, who was incapable of so unworthy an act, should dismiss the poor creature on account of ill health, to make it a point to do all that *humanity* required of him to promote her comfort. Thus did he seek ever to blind himself to the real motives that in certain particulars actuated his conduct. He formed immediately a pretext for paying her a visit, and in the plenitude of a deceiving self-love, he conceived, on regarding her, that her cheek looked

paler, and her form reduced. This idea
gave an additional victory to that slow
undermining power she was gaining over
his heart, and caused him, when he discovered the increasing interest which he
felt for her, to excuse himself with the
vain reflection, that she was a female
formed for a higher station than the one
in which fortune had placed her.

While her mean and treacherous influence was thus gaining ground in the
mind of Angelo, her conduct became
daily more insufferable to the pride
and feelings of Gabrielle. She at length
determined to dismiss her, but in consequence of her having been, as she believed, a tender nurse to Felix, she decided, first to inform Angelo of the various causes she had received from her
of provocation, and to ask his concurrence in her intention. Accordingly

she took the first opportunity of introducing the subject, expressing at the
same time her regret that the ingratitude of the woman at so late a period
of her service, should have induced her
reluctantly to entertain an ill opinion of
her heart. Ere she had half concluded,
Angelo interrupted her, and while his
conscience smote him for the thought
he cherished, he hastily exclaimed,
" Why not at once discard her ?"

" I intended to have informed you
such was my wish," observed Gabrielle.

" Why ask my concurrence, upon
such a trifle," he faltered with a slight
blush:—" do it—do it this instant, if
you choose."

Gabrielle, who could see in this nothing but most ready acquiescence in her

proposal, (for though she had sometimes
been obliged to think *severely* of Angelo, she had never yet thought *humbly*
of him,) dropped the subject as unworthy further discussion, simply resolv-
ing to put her purpose in immediate
execution. Thus in a few hours Milborough received orders to quit the
house; she only smiled at the mandate,
and prepared to obey with alacrity.
While she was busily employed, Angelo,
led by one of those impulses he never
knew how to resist, entered her apartment. Milborough, who had fully expected this visit, nevertheless affected
surprise, forgot as usual in what she
was engaged, and in the utmost agitation stood still. Angelo, scarcely conscious of the purport of his visit, regarded her with some embarrassment;
he felt humbled, and ashamed of the
situation in which he found himself, yet

knew not how to retract. Milborough
saw that an impellant was necessary ; she
raised her eyes to those of Angelo, and
casting them hastily down again, burst
into tears. This was sufficient for him,
man becomes reassured when he perceives
that the confusion of a woman is greater
than his own ; he approached Milborough, took her hand, and inquired the
cause of her distress.

"Oh, my lord, do not ask me," she
cried ; "am I not going to quit my beloved Felix? to quit you—your service,
my lord ?"

"And do you so much regret that,
Milborough," said Angelo, in a soothing voice. The tears of Milborough
redoubled, but she did not speak, for
she knew when to be silent. Angelo's
heart was softened by her seeming an-

guish; he raised to his lips the hand he
held, unworthy Angelo! and causing
Milborough to be seated, he said in the
low voice of a man who is conscious
that he is saying what he ought not,
" Grieve not, Milborough; be assured,
that although you quit this house, I
shall ever remember you with gratitude
for the—the tenderness you have evinced towards my son, and—and—"

" Talk not of gratitude to me, my
lord," cried Milborough with a sigh.

" Of love then, Milborough," cried
Angelo, with a smile. " But whither do
you go from hence? inform me at once,
for I hear Felix coming towards us."

" I hear him too, my lord," said Milborough with a timid glance; "and
since—since you deign to ask me of my

destination—I go to my sister, who re-
sides at ——" Felix drew nearer. Angelo approached his ear, and the rest
of her communication was whispered;
when, unwilling that just at this moment
Felix should behold him with Milborough, he glided hastily through the
door that led into the apartment where
first he had become debased by attending
to her. Miserable Angelo! how art thou
sunk, when even from the presence of
thy child, thou fliest in confusion!

Triumphing in the folly of the one, and
the misery she was preparing for the other,
the worthless Milborough quitted the
house of her benefactors, where for years
she had possessed all the comforts of polished life, and been cherished as the hum-
ble friend and well wisher of the family;
in return she had insulted the wife, seduced the husband, and corrupted the

child. Such too often is the return of the
depraved and mercenary vulgar for
favours received, on whom benefits make
no impression beyond the moment, and
in the vocabulary of whose sensations
the feeling, *gratitude* is not admitted.

A new æra of folly, or rather of vice, in
the life of Angelo, now presents itself; the
vice no longer of youth either, but of
maturer years, the most unworthy, the
most inexcusable, of all his former vices.
If in the seduction of Gabrielle might
be pleaded an impetuous love, excited
by her manifold perfections; if in forsaking such excellence, might be pleaded
his natural fickleness, allured by the
sprightliness and affected simplicity of
an Oriana ; if further outraging a love
and sentiments of which he was unworthy, he could presume to offer in exte-
nuation the ravishing beauty, youth,

and seeming innocence of a Paulina; what
could he urge, when neither youth,
grace, mind, nor manners, could be ad-
duced as the attraction ? What but a
cureless depravity of taste, which being
satiated by that which is good, seeks to
excite anew a sickly appetite, by a refer-
ence to that which is bad ?

Milborough possessed nothing, impar-
tially considered, to charm or to allure;
she was neither beautiful nor young,
nor from her birth and education could
she possibly be even elegant ; in all probability she would for ever have passed
unnoticed by Angelo, had she not intro-
duced herself to his attention by flattering his vanity. Instantly he discovered
in her a thousand charms, which she
possessed not, and which, but for that
single inducement, he never would have
conceived her to possess. Now he be-

came weary of the sameness of being virtuous, though he was only negatively so, and longed again for the meretricious pleasures of guilt.

Thus then, after the departure of the worthless Milborough, his feet wandered from home towards her habitation; her joy at beholding him, though decorously she desired to veil it, scarcely could be concealed from his view. The first decisive step once taken, the successive ones were easy, and followed rapidly; visit produced visit; from frequency, grew familiarity, from familiarity a fixed and settled intercourse that ultimately involved the most terrible consequences.

For a time Milborough continued to pay court to the weak side of Angelo, which her keen vulgar cunning had dis-

covered to be an inordinate vanity: this
mode of conduct had first drawn him
towards her, and now rivetted him, and
when at times his own polished education,
refined knowledge of customs, and propriety, would discover to him the gross
inaccuracies of Milborough, he would
excuse himself for being pleased with
her society in the fancied conviction of
her possessing an excellent heart, and
in the flattering belief that if he were
to abstain from seeing her, she would
die of grief. But when once a vulgar
mind gains an ascendancy over a weak
one, its obsequiousness ends, and the
fawning flatterer becomes a most insufferable tyrant; its requisitions are those
of profound folly, ignorance, and boundless presumption; and such trammels
are more difficult to be shaken off than
those of wisdom or of virtue.

Such was Milborough: she waited
patiently till she beheld her empire secure ; that it was so she ascertained by
increasing gradually her demands upon
Angelo; and finding each time that they
were complied with without a single remonstrance, although she well knew at
the time, they were such as he must
find it difficult to compass; for exam-
ple, among other things, she once desired
him to procure for her some jewels which
she remembered to have seen Gabrielle
wear, promising that she would return
them immediately that she had used
them once, and he might then replace
them from whence he took them, ere
Gabrielle could perceive that they
were missing. The imprudent Angelo
complied with this most insolent de-
mand, when to his confusion she afterwards laughingly refused to resign them,
and observing his embarrassment, vowed

like a fury that she was determined to keep them, or never see him more.

Angelo, in the true spirit of the libertine, who requires a zest even to what he loves, was terrified at this threat ; for though he might have endured a separation with indifference, had he found she trembled at the thought, yet when she became the instigator, he discovered in her charms which he had never seen before. But what resource had he in the dilemma in which he had unwarily involved himself? Unwilling to lead Gabrielle into the error of suspecting any one unjustly, unwilling to appear or to acknowledge himself a thief in her eyes, he had then only this alternative. He caused a set precisely similar to those he had deprived her of to be formed in paste, and replaced them in her cabinet ere, domestic and unadorned as she ever was, she had mis·

sed them. Oh.! passion, when indulged
for a worthless object, to what degradation wilt thou hurry man !

Mean time Gabrielle who had been for
some time in ignorance of this disgrace-
ful connexion, and who could not possibly suspect it, from having been accustomed to appreciate too highly the pride
and dignity of Angelo, now heard of it
from all with whom she had any ac-
quaintance, who scarcely even imagined
it a secret from her ; her own servants
were fully informed of the odious truth,
and though they seemed indignant at the
infamy of Milborough, and treated their
mistress with increased respect, it was
perhaps more from envy (which ever
exists among the vulgar against each
other) at the good fortune of the former,
than sincere and generous sympathy in
the outrage offered to the latter.

Indeed, the low minded Milborough did her utmost to impress upon the mind of Gabrielle, that these reports were far from being unfounded: she had an elegant establishment, and she disguised from no one, that it was the Count D'Albini who enabled her to support it; she had an equipage emblazoned with his arms, servants wearing his livery, and with these her base and insensible soul led her to parade in unblushing triumph past the door of her former mistress, in hopes of at some period attracting her attention. Sometimes she even carried her shameless audacity so far as to force into the seat beside her, the weak, degraded Angelo, who, fearing to refuse, was borne along to catch the view of her he was so cruelly insulting, yet not unblushing, but trembling like a culprit who hides his head, with shame, from the glance of a just judge.

D 3

Gabrielle saw, in silence saw, the career of Angelo, at a period of life when the wild horses of folly slacken their course, and reason, becoming powerful, calls them from the chace; when the soul desires to *rest* from vain and ignoble pursuits, and experiences in the calm of a reformed and virtuous life, more happiness than was ever found in the palling irrational excesses of youth. She lived in the firm and pious hope, that each day would convince him more deeply of his misconduct, and that better reason must speedily prevail over what she considered the last ebullitions of expiring error.

Bitter adversity, frequent disappointment, had so rationalized as it were the firm mind of Gabrielle, that she now considered events rather in a philosophical point of view, as resulting from an ine-

vitable necessity, and not therefore to be
deeply or vainly lamented. In the pride
of her youth and beauty, bitterly had
she felt the derelictions of Angelo ; but
now with a humility that rendered her
but more exalted, placing the rich trea-
sures of her mind from the question, and
estimating her personal charms even far
below their real standard, she remembered that she was no longer so young or so
attractive as formerly, and that the passions, tastes, and inclinations of men out-
living, from their habits and mode of
education, those of women, would sometimes lead them to pursue to a late period of life the means of indulging or gra-
tifying them, and that therefore they
were not to be too severely arraigned for
faults almost implanted in their nature.
Thus did she endeavour to excuse in Angelo, not only to herself, but to others, a
conduct for which all who knew her

despised and condemned him ; and this she did, still cherishing hope, that her patience, toleration, and forbearance, must have ere long its effect over a good and honest heart, which still, spite of his errors, she believed Angelo's to be. Neither could she think, as at first she could not credit *who* it was that had attracted Angelo, that an object so every way despicable could continue to detain him in the path of evil.

But when at length hope faded from her bosom, and still she perceived that his degradation continued; heart-sick and wretched, she shut herself up in her chamber ; and a native pride which few could understand, and which she inherited from her noble father, made her refuse to see any one whose pity must have humbled, and whose unfeeling condolence she would have deemed an insult. The unhappy Gabrielle perceived too soon, that in flattering herself the dreadful misconduct of Angelo would be but of short duration, she possessed not a just knowledge of human nature ; for the errors of later years are far more inveterate than those of youth. She perceived likewise that what little decorum he had for a time thought fit to observe towards her, and which had been with her indeed a strong ground of hope (for naturally, argued she, he is ashamed, and will not therefore persevere in what gives a feeling of humiliation) gradually wore off, and a bold insensibility of demeanour succeeded, not more cruel and unworthy, than it was offensive to delicacy and propriety. He was now seldom at home, he avoided as much as possible the sight of the injured Gabrielle, but if accidentally they met, he seemed impatient, and his manners were constrained, or coldly polite. What al-

ternative for her under circumstances
so hopeless ? She still remembered she
had a son; at some future period she might
be assured that she had still a daughter;
she decided then at once to remain un-
shaken, to *bear* and to *forbear* with the
father for the sake of his children.

Such was her resolution, a resolution,
as she conceived, of duty and necessity.
But soon she found that even on this
principle she might be justly exonerated from further endurance of the treatment of Angelo, from the sacrifice of
her best and tenderest feelings at the
shrine of that duty which had ever been
the invariable motive of all her actions,
and to which she was still willing to become a martyr.

The young Felix, who, as has been already observed, entertained for his supe-

rior mother but little affection, bestowed
all of that sentiment which he was capable
of feeling on the abandoned Milborough,
for whom he pined in secret, and whom
since her departure from the house he
had not seen. In vain did the unfortunate mother seek in the eyes of her son
for some shadow of respectfully tender
commiseration; in them she beheld,
often a restless roving expression, but
at all times an indifference to her. There
was no eloquent sympathy in the tone of
his voice ; in his manners, no soothing
gentleness; from him too was she compelled to turn with a deep drawn sigh
of anguish, but in that sigh *remembered*
that though unhappily he loved her
not, he was her son.

Such became the boundless and audacious extravagance of the worthless Milborough, whose aim it was as much to

reduce Angelo to beggary, to destroy
Gabrielle, as to enrich herself, that the
magnitude of her demands sometimes
anticipated, and even exceeded the re-
ceipts of Angelo. In his absence she
kept the lowest society, such as was
most consonant to her birth, ideas, and
former station, and indulged with them
in the most expensive and riotous ca-
rousals. As a man is rarely singly vicious, that is, vicious in a single point
alone, Angelo, to support and gratify
the unlimited profusion of this woman,
found an excuse for resorting with increased ardour to what had ever been a
favourite pursuit of his, the vice of
gaming: success had attended him often,
when as a pleasure merely he yielded
to the propensity, but now that he resorted to it as a mean, while Milborough was draining him on one hand,
this was impoverishing him on the other.

Loss succeeded to loss, and his perpetual
failure, so far from inducing him to withdraw, ere certain ruin should ensue, rendered him desperate, and caused him to
persevere, in the delusive hope, that one
fortunate throw would speedily retrieve
all. He was mistaken however; fortune,
fickle like himself, repaid him in kind,
and fled from him when most he court-
ed her.

It now remained only for the artful
Milborough, who had found the pliant
Angelo acceding, whether remonstra-
tingly or otherwise, but still acceding
to her every request, to propose to him
one which in insolence and depravity
should far exceed any which she had
hitherto proposed. It was not enough
for her, that by the most ruinous excesses, and shameless profligacy, she
was shortening the life of Gabrielle, as

she was abridging her means of existence, but she desired to injure her in a
deeper degree, or rather to destroy her
at once.

Aware that though she had weaned
the love of Felix from his mother, yet
aware likewise of her extravagant fondness for him, and considering that while
he was no longer in the sphere of her
attraction, nor capable of being contaminated by her influence, nature and
the exquisite goodness of his unhappy
parent might prevail in his heart, she
determined to deprive Gabrielle of him,
whom groundlessly she feared might
prove a consolation to her in her misery;
and for this purpose she demanded of
Angelo, in that flattering fawning tone
in which she usually solicited favours
of him, and which, strange to say, seldom failed of producing its effect, that

he would permit, as the highest gratification he could confer on her, that the
boy Felix might visit her for one day,
adding, " I know you will not refuse
me, my dearest Angelo : you never look
so captivating as when you grant my re-
quests." Angelo, with a pleased smile,
while he absolutely considered her the
most engaging female he had ever
known, replied that he would think of
what she required, secretly determining
in his mind, without the smallest compassion for the feelings of the insulted
Gabrielle, that he would surprise her
that very evening with the sight of her
favourite Felix.

Nothing could equal the sycophantic
insidiousness of Milborough, when she
wished to gain a point with Angelo, nothing her base deceit; she could be
compared only to the snake, which

gently coiling round the victim it wishes
to destroy, twists tighter and more
tight till its firm grasp can be no more
disputed, and agonizing death ensues.
Possessed of no internal dignity, no
high-mindedness, the most abject meanness of conduct conveyed no unpleasant
feeling to her heart: she flattered, and
fawned, and crouched, when desiring
a favour; she was arrogant, and daring,
and insufferable, when she had obtained
it—passing rapidly from the extreme
of slave to tyrant. But if by a most
unusual chance she did *not* immediately
obtain it, if Angelo dared to hesitate,
then she had another line of acting in
reserve; she ranted, stormed, and threat-
ened that if he did not instantly com-
ply, she would quit him suddenly, and
he should never hear of her more; thus
artfully bringing before him as a misfortune, that which would have been for

him the greatest good that could have
befallen.

Faithful to his intention, the degraded
Angelo left her for the purpose of returning to her with Felix. As the youth
was frequently a companion in his ram-
bles, to the edification neither of his
head nor heart, his going with him from
home excited no remark from Gabrielle,
but pleased her rather, from the so natural conviction that he could not be
going to Milborough.

Felix neither asked nor cared whither
he was going; he was going from home,
from under the same roof with his ever
melancholy mother, and his vivacity speedily revived, thoughtless and wild. Angelo made no observation with respect
to the object he had in view, till they
arrived at the door of an elegant habi-

tation ; as soon as they gained admit-
tance, he ran up stairs, bade Felix follow, and in a moment he was in the presence of Milborough, who receiving
him with open arms, scarcely knew how
to express the exuberance of her joy.

Felix was now happy, he was with
Milborough; he thought indeed she appeared less handsome, because less easy
than in her homely attire, but she was
more sprightly than his melancholy mother, and towards him at least was un-
altered. Too young accurately to understand, he yet surmised something of
the truth, and easily perceived that his
favourite Milborough was likewise, as
he had often wished her to be, a favourite with his father ; he looked upon her
as his *indulgent* mother, who never exerted over him any authority like his
severe one, as he had been taught to

consider the mild and gentle Gabrielle,
and who, if she could see him happy,
would never disapprove of the means by
which he became so.

The education of the youth, independ-
ently of his little application, was, through
the eternal procrastination and care-
lessness of Angelo, but very slightly im-
proved ; he feared to damp his young
energies by ponderous and oppressive
study, he remembered that he himself
had never been pestered with school
learning, and that he had parents (to
the full as inconsiderate towards him as
he was now towards his own son,) who
would not suffer him to quit home, or to
clog his sprightly genius, but procured
for him a private tutor, under whom he
made sufficient progress to qualify him
for the rank and situation he was to
hold in society ; while from his mother

he learnt affability and sweetness of
manners, from his father, polite and elegant demeanour. Such then he insisted
should alone be the education of Felix.
Thus is error transmitted from father to
son, and frequently perpetuated to the
destruction of successive generations.
A private tutor, Angelo observed, might
be always obtained; mean time he could
himself impart to his son some necessary
instruction, and it was useless to deprive himself so precipitately of an en-
tertaining companion and pleasing associate, of whom he was so extravagantly
fond.

Thus, then, on Gabrielle devolved the
task of fitting his young mind for future
study, by imbuing it with a love of science and thirst of further knowledge.
The stores of her own rich and elegantly
fraught mind, fraught by the delicate

and careful hand of a father, she desired to impart to her son, and fully ade-
quate was she to the task: but Felix
soon perceiving that no one but her attempted to restrain him, (for Angelo,
unmindful even of his own arrangement,
had no *letsure* as yet to give instructions which he could at *any time* impart,) and that his avocations with his
mother detained him frequently from a
pleasurable excursion with his father,
or from some entertainment prepared for
him by Milborough, conceived, from
the imprudence and improper conduct
of those around him, a disgust for study, which, at the insinuations of the domestic traitor, Milborough, who might
have differently exerted her influence,
was easily transferred into a dislike of
her who taught. Thus, from the pecu-
liarly unfortunate situation in which she
was placed, Gabrielle perceived by slow

degrees, and with an anguish inexpressible, her power over the mind of her son on the wane; he no longer attended to her implicitly, or if she succeeded in rivetting him for a moment, Angelo would too frequently call him off for some more agreeable, but more unprofitable pursuit. Felix by these means was induced rather to shun than court her society; and, in dismay at finding herself the only tyrant of the youth, her firm perseverance relaxed, for she felt that those instructions must be useless which were never received but with reluctance. Thus was a fine field left open for the suggestions of ignorance and depravity; for where wisdom and virtue were not suffered to take root, the weeds of error sprang up apace.

Milborough had asked of Angelo that he would permit Felix for *once* to visit

her ; but her request only literally grant-
ed, would not have answered her purpose; she therefore having obtained possession of the youth, would no more suffer
him to depart, but assured Angelo laughing, that having long this idea in view,
she had had an apartment in readiness
for him, for some time past. Angelo was
confounded; he declined entering into any
dispute with Milborough before his son,
but flattered himself that he should
easily prevail upon her to give up so in-
decorous and extravagant a caprice at
another opportunity.

Mean time Felix, rejoiced to excess,
was permitted to remain, and the abandoned Milborough carried as usual her
point.

CHAPTER XX.

THE unhappy Gabrielle, immured almost always in her solitary chamber, worn out, and nearly heart-broken with ceaseless suffering and disappointment, felt that with her intellectual energy so long upheld, (but now rapidly sinking) her physical strength was decaying likewise, and that long thus she could not continue to exist. The few who, attracted by her singular worth and merits, had *made it a point* to call themselves her friends, captivated more by the desire of appearing liberal and high minded than from any real admiration they were capable of feeling, she had from the humiliating dereliction of Angelo refused to see, for they had been his friends before they had professed themselves hers; and her genuine sense of delicacy and honour shrunk from the impropriety of hearing animadversions passed upon him on her account, or from the contemptible meanness of seeking to inspire pity by the gentle resignation with which she endured insults, that she could have wished unknown for ever to any but herself.

Thus, she was almost isolated. Angelo she scarcely ever saw, and Felix when in her presence appeared not employed by any thought so much as that of escaping from it. Now, of beholding even him sometimes, she suddenly found herself deprived; where could he be? A dreadful idea glanced across her mind,

he must be with his father.—should she
condescend to inquire of the servants if
he had returned and departed again
alone?—No, to no eye could she voluntarily betray her grief, and mortifying
ignorance of the movements of those so
near to her.   She determined then to
preserve silence, but vigilantly to watch
for the moment when Felix should make
his appearance, and question himself as
to whither he had been.

But in vain she was silent, in vain she
watched.   Felix appeared no more. The
anguish of her mind became intense, she
felt almost certain *where* he lingered, and
had half determined to address Angelo by letter upon this dreadful subject,
when with his usual constrained air he
suddenly appeared before her.

"Angelo," exclaimed she, starting up,

the moment she beheld him, incapable
of restraining her emotion, while he
cooly bowed; "Angelo, oh! let us wave
all idle ceremonies for the present, I
am too sick to attend to them, tell me,
and tell me truly I beseech you, where
is my son?—*your son*—?"

"Really, Gabrielle, this is such an extraordinary salute that—that I,"—he
stopped embarrassed.

"Oh! Angelo," cried the distracted
Gabrielle, seizing him by the arm—"away
with this mockery, and answer me at
once—This suspense is worse than the
most dreadful certainty; tell me what
have you done with Felix?"

"This conduct is so singular, madam,
that really—"

"Oh God!" interrupted Gabrielle, clasping her hands, and bursting into tears "is it thus then that you treat me, Angelo!—But no matter," she pursued, endeavouring to throw firmness into her voice, and to collect herself; "inform me only of my son—1 claim a *right*, sir, to be informed upon that subject."

Angelo was awed, and shrank into himself; he felt that Gabrielle had justice on her side, and that he had not. Like a culprit summoned before a judge, comes to defend a bad cause, and seeing his accuser before him is struck dumb by the power of conscience—so Angelo, when he raised his eyes to the accusing form of the injured Gabrielle, felt how truly guilty he was, and remained silent. Gabrielle, uttered no reproach; she determined not to utter any, for she felt their inutility, since he who is not just from

inclination, will never be rendered so by
the voice of reproof; but finding that he
still preserved a confused silence, she in
a firm voice repeated her question.

"He is under my care," at length stam-
mered Angelo.

"Not at present," observed Gabrielle.

"He is safe," said Angelo.

"Convince me," answered Gabrielle.—

"My word is surely sufficient."

"Not in the present case; you will not,
my lord, lay your hand upon your heart,
and say that you consider him at *this*
moment where he ought to be."

Angelo was silent; he looked aside. Gabrielle fixed on his varying countenance her sad, yet searching eyes, and uttered in a voice of solemn anguish,

"He is with *Milborough.*"

Angelo started, as if in horror that it *should be so*—so true is conscience. He made no reply.

"Your silence is sufficient confirmation," pursued she in the same impressive tone : "now then, Angelo, ere it be too late, return him to me."

'That cannot be," said Angelo.

"Cannot be !—cannot be !" shrieked Gabrielle, again overpowered by the violence of her feelings—"Oh Angelo, Angelo," she continued, falling on her knees,

and raising her clasped hands towards
him, " I conjure you, not by your present
love, but by the love you once had for
me,—I conjure you for the future welfare and happiness of your child,—if you
consider aught that is most valuable to
him in existence—I implore, I beseech
you, let him not remain with *that*
woman :—destruction, yes eternal destruction must ensue, not only of present
but of future life—his *soul* will be sacrificed. Angelo, I implore you listen to
my prayer, return him to me ere he be
lost beyond redemption."

The heart of Angelo throbbed violently—he was affected by her solemn
adjuration, but he desired not that she
should perceive it; he looked at Gabrielle for a moment, he durst not longer,—
he endeavoured to raise her from the
ground as with averted face he said,

" In aught else command me, Gabrielle; but the boy must remain where he is."

" Then !" cried Gabrielle, springing from her knees with a countenance of fire, and looking sternly upon Angelo, " *Then his destruction be upon your head;* remember, that at a *future* day, you will *curse* yourself for this !—remember—remember—that *he* will curse you likewise !"

" Frantic woman !" cried Angelo, roused to a consciousness of guilt, and therefore of rage, at her awful prophecy, " Frantic woman ! he is my son—I have a right to do with him as I will, and who dare dispute my pleasure?"

" His *mother*," answered Gabrielle in a firm voice, " *she* dares—sir, he is *my*

son as well as yours, and I have as dear
an interest in him !"

"Yes," interrupted Angelo, with a
bitter smile, "more than *he* has in you.!"

"The more my misfortune ! the more
my misfortune !" cried the wretched
Gabrielle in a voice of anguish, and
bursting into tears, "Cruel Angelo, I
little expected this reproach from *you*;
but still I will spare you."

Angelo, shocked at the observation
that had escaped him, detesting himself for his unworthy cruelty, found his
feelings of bitterness increased by his
self-contempt, and hastily cried, "Well,
madam, this scene is unnecessarily prolonged, I have other avocations."

"Ah yes, too well do I know that you

have; but hear me a moment," she pursued, endeavouring to subdue her suffocating emotion, " hear me but a moment. Since I may not be permitted to claim my son, to be considered as the mother of my child, grant me but this, for surely you will not deny me all. Suffer me once more to behold him, let me take of him a last farewell, it may enable me to exist a little longer under this most cruel misery.

" Well," said Angelo, who though he had not been generous enough to concede for his past unfeeling insinuation, yet desired to make some amends, " Well, be it so then ; I will bring him to you presently."

" Let me see him alone."

" Promise me then that you will not attempt to tamper with the boy."

" *I tamper* with him !"

" That you will not offer to detain
him then."

" I *promise*," said Gabrielle, while a
tear struggling from its confinement,
fell hastily down her cheek, " I promise that he shall do nothing unwil-
lingly."

" Well, that conditional promise will
do," observed Angelo, while the inconsiderate remark conveyed an added pang.
to the lacerated heart of the mother.
Angelo prepared to depart ; she sought
not to detain him, and he left the room,
promising that she should presently behold her son.

Slight was the hope which Gabrielle
ventured to cherish from this promised

interview ; her sole dependance was on
the power she might possess of working on
the feelings of the youth ; though he loved
her not, she determined to leave no means
untried to snatch him from destruction ;
the cruel remarks of Angelo, indeed, left
no room for sanguine reliance, and
while her conscience proudly whispered
to her, that she had done every thing to
deserve the fondest affection of Felix,
she felt that even the consciousness of
virtue abates not the pang which is inflicted on the heart of a mother by a
child's ingratitude.

The slavish and degenerate Angelo, returning to Milborough, almost feared to inform her of the promise into which he had
entered ; but at length he found courage
carelessly to insinuate that Felix must
return home with him immediately. No
sooner had he spoke than he beheld all

the fury gathering in the countenance
of Milborough ; she repeated the word
" home" contemptuously, and vowed
that the youth should not be suffered to
quit her presence, even for an instant.

But the word of Angelo was pledged,
and subject as he was, he resolved to
abide by it, and for once even to assert
himself; he therefore retorted upon Milborough, expressing that his pleasure
should be obeyed, who had immediate
recourse to her usual violence upon all
occasions when Angelo presumed to op-
pose her. In a passion of rage he exclaimed, that as she had obtained possession of the boy by fraud and artifice,
she should not be permitted to detain
him by presumption and violence, and
that if she persisted in her present opposition, he would not only depart with

him immediately, but she should never
behold him more.

No sooner had Angelo spoken thus,
than the fury sunk into tame submission;
she wept, and attributed her warmth, as she
termed it, to the ardent affection which
she bore the youth, and her fears of
trusting him out of her presence, lest by
some unforeseen event she should be deprived of him for ever ; she concluded
by imploring of Angelo, that if he
determined to fulfil his purpose, he
would first suffer her to be a few minutes
alone with her beloved Felix. To this
the imprudent Angelo readily assented.
The youth, who had witnessed the alter-
cation respecting him, and who secretly
hoped that Milborough would prove
triumphant, accompanied her with alacrity from the room.

She employed the moments allowed
her by Angelo in steeling him to the
dreaded influence of his mother, and
exhorting him not to be *seduced* by her
pretended fondness and eloquent speeches;
for the wretched Milborough was well
aware of her own vulgar incapacity,
and that every triumph she gained over
the heart of Felix was obtained by means
most vile and reprehensible. " Do not,
my dear lovely Felix," added she in her
illiterate jargon, " let yourself be prevailed upon by fair promises and fine
acting to live again with your mother,
for you know well how she used to damp
your spirits, and check you, my dear
boy, till my heart bled for you, and she
could never bear to see you happy. It
would be all the same again in a little
time, and you would wish yourself in
your grave before the end of a month.
Nobody, my dearest Felix, loves you as

I do, and *nobody never* can, not even
your father ;—all my happiness is to see
you happy." She pursued in a faltering
voice, and calling in the aid of tears,
which she suffered to trickle down her
cheeks, that their effect might not be lost
upon the youth, " and I am certain if
you do not return to me, I shall die of
grief ; I feel it."

The youth embraced her with an affection due only to a mother, and vowed
that he would return to her, loving her
as he did a thousand times better than
his natural parent : indeed his sentiments were too much in unison with
those of his infamous adviser ; she had
taught him to consider his mother, not
only with the utmost disrespect, but as
a severe and implacable judge, from
whom it was requisite to conceal the innocent indulgences which she bestowed

upon him; as a harsh overseer of every
pleasure, which as requiring none herself, she thought unnecessary for youth;
he was taught, in short, to regard her as
an enemy, rather than a friend; and a
capricious tyrant, rather than an anxious mother. Above all, the vile Milborough failed not to impress upon his
mind, what she had so often laboured
to effect, that his mother was no more
entitled to his veneration, from the
purity of her conduct, or her esteemed
rank in society, than she was to his affection, for her kindness or indulgence;
adding, that she was now far inferior,
even to herself, inasmuch as the Count
D'Albini no longer considered her as
his wife. Thus prepared with hypo-
critical caresses, and manifestations of
regret, she suffered him to depart with
Angelo, who had begun to grow impatient, purely from the desire of getting

rid of an affair, in which he now regret-
ted to have involved himself. He accompanied the youth to the door of his
insulted mother, without making to him
any other observation than that when
she permitted him to depart, he should
expect to see him again, where of late
he had resided. To this remark, Felix promised acquiescence, with an eagerness that embarrassed and somewhat
shocked even Angelo: then, faithful to
his agreement, of not being present at
the interview, when the door opened he
waved his hand, and left him.

Felix walked leisurely up stairs, for-
getting, in the indifference or rather reluctance with which he performed his
task, the animation so natural to youth.
Gabrielle who had been passing the in-
termediate space in the most painful
anxiety, had heard his arrival, and heard

his subsequent slow step upon the stairs,
which struck upon her ear as the knell
of death, and nearly deprived her of the
slight portion of hope and firmness
which she had been endeavouring to
acquire.

The door opened, the youth bowed
slightly and advanced. Gabrielle half
rose from her chair, to meet him; but
his cool and settled countenance, his un-
affectionate air, checked her instantly, and
again she sank down, merely stretching
forth to him her trembling hand, which
partaking the agitation of her whole
frame, was covered with a cold dew.
Felix approached, and took her hand;
he retained it for a moment; he neither
pressed nor carried it to his lips, but
remained standing beside her, though
with an air embarrassed, yet devoid of

the least symptom of tenderness or sensibility.

The anguished mother fixed her eyes upon his youthful countenance, so youthful yet so hard to her,—upon that countenance on which so often she had gazed with fond delight, so fair, so health blooming, surrounded in graceful luxuriance by bright auburn curls, while her's, sad contrast, was pale as death itself; an unwiped tear rested upon her frozen cheek, she resembled a broken down lily upon which some remains of the torrent that bowed it to the earth still hangs. Her son raised his eyes to that face in which sadness and despair were so vividly depicted ; he raised his eyes, but cast them down again slowly— his *heart* was unmoved.

" Felix, my dear child," said the anguished mother, in a low voice, for she durst not grant it its usual latitude, " will you not speak to me ?"

" I thought it was you, who desired to speak with me," returned Felix.

" But, my dear love, after so long an absence, have you not any thing to say to me?"

" Not so *very* long an absence," returned the youth with an insensible smile, which was answered by a deep-drawn sigh from the heart of the mother, she endeavoured to command herself, however, and said—

" Have you been happy then, my dear Felix, since the time appears so short to you?"

" Oh, yes, indeed," replied Felix, his vivacity returning, " I was never so happy before."

" And could you not be equally happy with me ?"

Felix was silent.

" Could you not be happy, my child, with a mother who tenderly loves you ?"

" You are always so melancholy."

" But I would endeavour to be cheerful," answered Gabrielle, waving, in her anxiety to detach her son from his present ruinous situation, his unfeeling remarks upon herself.

" Ah ! but," said Felix, " Milborough,"—he stopped, confused, having

involuntarily uttered her name, which a
certain feeling convinced him he ought
not to have done.

"Well, what of her?" said Gabrielle
in an irregular voice, yet affecting not
to notice his confusion.

"Why she," answered Felix venturing to look up, "she is always so
kind."

"She was a kind nurse to you, my
child, but she has not those claims upon
you that I have. Do you not remember,
before you even knew her, when you
were extremely young, how fond you
were of me? the care I took of you,
how I studied your happiness, your
pleasure?" Tears hindered her from pro-
ceeding, for at that moment she remembered the bleak wintry night when, wan-

dering about with him in her arms, fa-
mishing herself that he might be sus-
tained, supporting him from the wet
ground when having scarcely strength
to support herself, how he smiled upon
her, and caressed her as in fond gratitude for her kindness, now to look upon
her so changed! so insensible! turning
aside from her, who had endured
so much for him—him who had been
her primary care, her object in every
movement. Scarce could she persuade herself that she beheld before her this cherished darling son, disputing for his love
with a hired mercenary wretch, whom
unblushingly he acknowledged to prefer
to *her!* The thought was agony, was
horror, and she wept aloud.

Felix observed her intense anguish,
but he made no effort to allay it ; so estranged was his heart from her, that he

knew not *how*, nor did he feel a sensation sufficiently strong to induce him to
make the attempt; he experienced impatience only, at witnessing a grief by
which he was unaffected, and which
cast a gloom over moments that might
have been more pleasingly employed.

"Great God!" cried Gabrielle, as
she gazed on him through her tears,
and marked his stubborn averted countenance, and eye which roved around,
"great God! how has the heart of this
child become thus hardened towards his
mother?—what fiend-like influence can
have corrupted him thus in so short a
time? for no human power could have
worked a change so rapid and prodi-
gious."

Unhappy Gabrielle! she knew not that
this had been no work of a moment, nor

that his love, respect, and filial feelings
towards her had been for years undermining by the base intrigues of a remorseless
destroyer. Grief, anguish, compassion,
were the predominant sensations of her
mind; she felt not anger, but acute regret at witnessing the unyielding insensibility of the youth, and as he still
stood beside her, she threw her arms
around him, and shed over him *tears
too bitter* to be the portion of a *mother !*
Felix did not struggle to withdraw himself from her embrace, neither did he
return it—she looked at him, but his
eyes were tearless, while on his cheek,
wet only with those *she* had shed, man-
tled a faint conscious blush.

Gabrielle now felt the full hopeless-
ness of her struggle, she relaxed in despair her fond embrace, for she perceived
by his faint blush that though he was sen-

sible to his conduct, he still persevered in it: yet suddenly she exclaimed, "Yes, you must, you shall remain with me, Felix! it is for your good that you should, it is my duty to command it, it is yours to obey. This cruel reserve, this insensibility towards a mother will subside: my anxious care, my love, shall make it! My dearest child, say you will remain with me; you shall have no cause to repent."

"But you say it is my duty," observed Felix, the poison of Milborough's base principles fermenting in his mind: "it is not my *duty*."

"Well then, my love, forget the term, be it inclination," cried Gabrielle, regarding him with tearful eyes, willing upon any terms to save him from compleat destruction.

F 2

"But it is not my *duty*," pursued the unhappy child, "more to remain with you, than with Milborough."

"Certainly, my child, more with me; she was only your nurse, I am your mother; she is not wedded to your father, she is not"——

"Neither are *you*!—she says,"—cried Felix interrupting her.

This was too much; the heart-stricken Gabrielle, uttering a faint exclamation, sprang up, her pale cheek glowing with the deepest crimson; her soul shook within her, and though scarcely had she the power to stand, with a desperate effort she summoned her receding strength and rushed half frantic from the room. Scarce had she gained her own apartment ere she fell prostrate on the floor, and

kind insensibility gave a temporary relief
to nature from pangs which with life
it could not long have borne.

Felix, whose feelings were not refined
either by nature or education, did not
conceive, when he saw his mother rush
from the room, that what he had last
uttered could have produced such an
effect. His stubborn silence had been
now broken, and he rather expected from
her some reply; for a short time he remained in the apartment she had so
abruptly quitted, supposing that she
would speedily return, and fearing to
go unbidden lest he should be again subject to a future similar interview. When
however he found that she neither returned, nor sent any one to him, he considered himself at liberty to depart, and
without further hesitation running down
the stairs, though he had only walked up,

he felt, when from beneath the roof of
his injured mother, his constraint va-
nishing, and his vivacity returning; while
the joy with which he rushed into the
house of Milborough, formed a forcible
contrast to the reluctant step with which
he had entered hers.

The abandoned Milborough received
him with an exultation that she could
not disguise; he related to her the issue
of his visit, and all that had passed during
its continuance; for the conduct he described himself to have pursued, he received from her profuse caresses, and
unbounded expressions of gratitude, for
preferring her to his mother, and for
having so faithfully kept his promise of
returning to her.

CHAPTER XXI.

A LITTLE time elapsed, and the change-
ful Angelo, steady only in his fickleness,
became gradually less bigotted to the
society of the uneducated Milborough,
and more addicted to his favourite habit
of gaming, and which, as has been before observed, in consequence of his
boundlessly increased expences, he now
resorted to, as much for profit as pleasure. But fortune grew daily more un-
kind; she still fled, he still pursued, and
in the true spirit of a gamester, he determined that he would not desist from
the chace while he retained the power

F 4

of continuing it, or if he felt his courage
on the wane, he recruited it by plentiful
libations to the rosy god.

One night, having lost to a consider
able amount, goaded on by rage, by a
despairing hope, and that resistless im-
pulse which ever actuates the real gamester, he drank off a bumper of the Tus-
can juice, and then, inspired with a false
courage, determined in a phrenzy, to
push fortune to the utmost, and not to
quit the table whilst a possibility of
staking aught remained, till he had endeavoured at least to cover the whole of
his losses.   He persevered, he was reso-
lute, and his resolution cost him dear ;
he staked to the amount of every guinea
he possessed, he followed it up by all
he could call his. the house in which
Gabrielle still continued to drag on her
lingering   existence,   his   equipages,

horses, plate, &c. and it was not till
he discovered that nothing more remained which he had a right to stake, (for
the house in which Milborough resided
was not his,) that he recovered his
senses to lose them again almost immediately in madness of a different description, and to rush a pennyless beggar from
the abode of ruin which late as that very
night he had entered in comparative
affluence.

The chief of his property had been lost,
or rather transferred to one person—that
person *his dearest and most intimate
friend*, one with whom he had sometimes
played with success, but more frequently to manifest disadvantage; he was steady,
politic, and cool, and found it no difficult
matter generally to come off conqueror
from one who was rash, inconsiderate,
without sufficient judgment to direct,

and without patience to abide by the
little he possessed. This friend, who,
though a man of the world, possessed
some feeling, perceiving the confusion
and horror of Angelo painted in his
countenance, seized him by the hand, and
cordially shaking it, bade him not let
dame Fortune obtain a victory over the
spirit of his soul, adding that he might
settle the affair between them at his lei-
sure, as it was furthest from his wish to
trouble or *inconvenience* him.

Such the language of the world, such
the consolation of their friendship ; and
even Ellesmere, the successful gamester,
possessed a greater share of feeling than
usually belongs to that class of beings,
who not only remorselessly strip each
other of all they possess, but attempt
neither to hide their exultation nor
speak a word of consolation, however
vain, to the wretch they have driven

to ruin and desperation. In a state of
madness, such however as left him of
sense sufficient to feel his woe, Angelo
reached the only spot which strictly
speaking he might presume to enter, the
abode of Milborough; he rushed into the
room, where she was sitting carelessly
singing an air with Felix ; one hand he
pressed to his burning forehead, the other
was stretched wildly towards them, as
bidding them cease ; his glazed eyes wandered around, his cheek glowed with a
feverish red, his brow was writhed, his
hair dishevelled, his vest torn open, and
his whole appearance the wildest image
of frenzy and despair, personified in the
ruined gamester ;

" For Heaven's sake, what has happened, Angelo?" exclaimed Milborough,
starting up. Angelo made no reply, but

gazing on her, burst into a convulsive
laugh.

"Good God! he is certainly mad,"
cried the unfeeling Milborough, rushing
toward the bell.

"Stay, Milborough," he exclaimed,
violently seizing her arm, roused by her
remark, and the action which accompanied it," I am not yet quite mad, but I
soon shall be; I am ruined, stripped of
every guinea I possess; I have not," he
cried, raising his voice to frenzy, "no,
I have not wherewithal to procure *bread*
for to morrow,"—and at the horri-
ble conviction, his eyes rolled wildly
round.

At this explanation the countenance
of Milborough suddenly changed, her
selfish terrors gave place to other ideas,

but no less selfish ; had Angelo spoken
for ever, he could not have said *more to*
her than was confirmed in the few words
he had uttered in the short sentence, " *I
am ruined !*" After the pause of a moment,
her countenance again underwent a
change, she drew near him ; and taking
his hand she said, " Is this all, my dearest Angelo ?"

" All!—all!" interrupted Angelo, " is
it not enough ?"

" Certainly it is dreadful, but not sufficient to throw you into despair. One
lucky cast might yet retrieve all, per
haps."

" Woman !" raved Angelo, " have I
not told you that I am beggared ! that
I have no longer a claim to the chance of
another cast !—or—or do you think I

would, like a *coward*, have retreated?"
added he, breathing the desperate defi-
ance of the gamester.

" Well, well, my dearest Angelo, com-
pose yourself, a glass of wine will do you
service. Fly, Felix, and procure some
wine for my lord,"

Angelo with a desponding groan threw
himself into a chair ; wine was brought,
Milborough poured him out a full
goblet, and presenting it to him, entreated that he would drink ; fevered with
heat, and his mouth parched, mechani-
cally he took the wine, and swallowed
it.

By dint of persuasion she prevailed
on him to drink a second glass, a third
and fourth then rapidly followed : from
the madness of despair, Angelo was pass-

ing fast into the madness of intoxication!
his cares began to assume an aspect less
terrific, and the exhilirating hope
which is inspired by wine, caused the
future to appear less gloomy ; by degrees
his moody despondency vanished, and, as
had been the secret aim of Milborough,
he applied spontaneously to the bottle
for that seducing influence, which sweetly blinded him to the frightful reality of
his situation.

Milborough now ventured carelessly
to revert to it :" But, my dear Angelo,"
she observed, " surely every thing is not
as bad as you think ; you have sufficient,
I trust, to cover all ; then you might retire upon a little."

" Upon nothing, you mean ! I can
never redeem myself."

" But, my lord," cried Felix, " could
you not collect all you have at present
in your possession, and make your escape to the Continent ?"

Angelo, nearly intoxicated, irritable,
and still alive to a certain sense of honour, looking fiercely at his son, seized
him by the arm, and for the first time
in his life inflicted on him a blow, and
inflicted it unjustly, for assuredly it was
no fault in the youth, that education had
not instilled into him proper principles,
or given him correct ideas.

He did not speak; his young heart
swelled with indignant fury, he looked
at his father with flashing eyes, and face
of fire ; it was the first correction he
had ever received; it was violent, and he
had never been accustomed tó any ; he
knew not how to endure it, he was burst-

ing to resent! a feeling of fear alone re-
strained him, and tears of impotent rage
rushed to his eyes! Milborough glanced
at him significantly, and affecting not
to notice the violence of Angelo, observed, " But you have money to a
large amount in the house, that you received from your banker the other day,
that surely may be saved, and at all events
will——"

" I must have that too ; all will be
insufficient."

" But you forget how much it is; lend
me the key of your cabinet, and I will
bring it to you."

" Do you suppose it has *increased*
since I placed it there?" cried Angelo,
throwing down the key, " I know too
well that all will be insufficient."

" Well," said Milborough, carelessly taking up the key, which she twisted round her finger, " it will at all events be a satisfaction to calculate ;" so saying she went towards the door, when suddenly returning, she exclaimed, " But I forgot, I must not leave you, Angelo, I shall have you getting gloomy again ; come, take another glass of wine, and banish care."

Angelo heaved a sigh, and hastily drank off the wine ; then leaning his head upon his hand, he remained absorbed in gloomy silence : he had returned, harassed, fatigued, exhausted, at an unusually late hour ; it was now getting dawn; his eyes were closed, his ideas became confused, his heavy head dropped from his hand, and he fell into a profound slumber.

No sooner did Milborough perceive that the wine had taken its desired
effect on him, than silently she rose and
beckoned Felix, (who was sternly brood-
ing over the blow he had received,) from
the room. Rising, involuntarily with
caution, he followed her out.

" Go," said Milborough in a whisper,
" if any of the servants remain up, tell
them they may retire, afterwards come
to me to the chamber of your father."

Felix left her, to act as she had desired, while she, hastening to the chamber
of Angelo, remained at the door waiting
his return. In a few moments Felix appeared ; Milborough placed her finger
on her lip, and in a low voice he said,
" I found only one servant up, and he
was in so deep a sleep that I could not
awake him."

" I am sorry you attempted it," said
Milborough, hastening as lightly as she
could down the stairs to the room where
Felix informed her the servant was sleeping; and then gently locking the door upon
him, retraced her steps to the chamber
of Angelo, still accompanied by Felix.
Having entered, she closed the door;
approaching his cabinet, she coolly un-
locked it, and taking thence all the gold
she could find, together with jewels to a
considerable amount, among which were
those that had appertained to Gabrielle,
and which she had obtained from Angelo by fraudulent artifice, she gave
them into the hands of Felix, saying,
" Let us at all events secure these from
the Count's creditors ; it would be a pity
they should obtain all : as for these
jewels they are mine, and they have no
right to them."

Felix acquiesced readily in her idea, and accepted the things from her hands. "Now then," said she, "Felix, be light and cautious; descend the stairs—for we quit this house for ever."

"Whither to go?" inquired Felix.

"Far from hence, but where we shall be safe."

"And my father?" cried Felix, half anxiously, half resentfully.

"He will *follow* us, perhaps : but did he not strike you just now, without provocation? why inquire about him? trust to me, my dear boy, and let us go at once."

Felix frowned, and blushed with indignant shame, at the recollection. "It *was* without provocation," said he, and hesitated no longer.

Milborough stepped lightly towards her chamber; she wrapped herself in a cloak which covered her entirely, and divested her dress of all attraction; she then proceeded down stairs with almost breathless caution. Felix followed; they reached the hall; Milborough remained a moment to secure about her own person the jewels with which she had loaded him, then silently unlocking the door she closed, without venturing to shut it, and proceeded with rapid pace along the street.

As it was the height of summer, and perfectly light at an early hour, they passed along completely unnoticed and unopposed. The object of Milborough was to get by the quickest possible con-

veyance to Dover, to arrive ere suspicion
could surmise her route, and from thence
embarking for the Continent, her fears of
pursuit would be at an end. In all
she had proposed, she succeeded even
beyond her most sanguine speculations;
she reached Dover, early, and without
interruption, and a little time after found
herself in perfect safety on the shores
of France. Here, for a time, with her
youthful and misguided companion, let
us leave her, and return to the wretched
but justly punished Angelo.

A few hours after the departure of
Milborough, he was awakened by a violent noise; opening his heavy eyes, he
found himself lying on the floor, and the
expiring flame of a taper burning in
the socket and emitting a faint irregular
light through the closed apartment.

The noise which had roused him still
continuing, he instinctively started up, and
hastened towards the spot from whence
it seemed to proceed : it was a loud
knocking, and appeared to come from the
lower offices of the house ; he followed
the sound, and soon discovered that it was
occasioned by his servant, who awaking
in alarm, and endeavouring to quit his
situation for the purpose of retiring to
bed, found his intention frustrated by
his inability to open the door, which had
been fastened upon him ; in consequence
of this discovery, conceiving robbers
were, or had been in the house, in the
greatest trepidation he had essayed his
utmost to make himself heard. Angelo
having emancipated him, began to recover his senses ; he now clearly remembered that he had not been in bed
for the night, but could by no means reconcile to himself why he should have

been suffered to remain asleep upon the
ground, alone too, and not have been conveyed to bed. His whirling head informed
him that he had drank inordinately, and he
concluded, that overpowered with sleep,
he had fallen on the floor. But as this
was a circumstance by no means unfre-
quent with him, and he was in such
cases always attended carefully to bed,
why had he been now abandoned
with this most singular neglect and indifference?

Rage began to kindle in his bosom,
and hastily he sought the chamber of
Milborough, to upbraid her in the severest terms for the impropriety of her
conduct, and the want of regard she
had evinced for him. He had questioned
the servant with respect to his confinement, but receiving from him only the most
unsatisfactory replies, that he neither

knew nor could surmise, he dismissed him
with intemperate revilings for his stu-
pidity, and hastened to the chamber of
Milborough, expecting from her explanation of this circumstance and of
her own apparently unfeeling neglect.

Entering her room, with an exclamation
of reproach on his lips, he perceived
immediately that she was not there, nor
had even been in bed! For a moment,
he stood amazed, then swifty retreating,
sought his own apartment, unknowing
what to expect. There the first and only
object which struck him, was his cabinet open, and its assemblage of drawers
dragged out to their fullest extent, and
completely empty! At this alarming
sight involuntarily he struck his forehead with his clenched hand, as an idea,
too dreadful to indulge, glanced like
lightning through his brain! He rushed

trembling towards the cabinet, examined it nearer, brought every drawer completely forth, and cast them on the ground, as if he desired some stronger confirmation than visual sense could give him of the dreadful view which presented itself! It was but too true; he found indeed that he had been plundered of all they contained, and, aghast with horror, he stood for a moment unable even yet to credit that he was perfectly awake.

All his gold, his jewels, even to a far greater amount, had vanished ! his dreadful situation, stern and unrelenting, was revealed before him, and with a bitter cry, rushing from the room, he flew into every apartment, loudly vociferating the name of Milborough, and hoping still, in the midst of his despair, that in some remote corner of the house he might yet discover her, even though

manacled, and dying perhaps for assistance; all, any thing, but that she should
have fled in a moment like the present!

In vain he called, in vain he searched,
Milborough answered not; his fears then
reverted to his son; he sought his chamber, he was not there either, he replied
not to his agonized repeated call; then
sinking overpowered on a chair, he
clasped his hands in horror; the whole
truth, the fearful truth, broke without
mercy and without reserve upon his
mind; no longer could he doubt *Milborough* was his plunderer, his *son* the
companion of her flight!

While thus he remained, the servant
he had with anger so unjust dismissed,
rushed into the room, and with a countenance of terror, observed that he had
discovered the door of the hall to be

open, that he apprehended the worst, but had not courage to search the house alone. "Go, go—I know," cried the sick and fainting Angelo, "I know all—retire."

The wild abstraction of his air alarmed the servant, who precipitately obeyed, and left the room. Gloomily musing, he still remained immoveable; ruin was certain, it could not be accumulated, nothing now could make it more than ruin, and he felt in that state, when the mind, conscious it has reached the climax of woe, is incapable from that dreadful consciousness of dreading aught as an increase.

Such are the retributions the guilty experience from the guilty, such the rewards of the libertine for yielding up his soul to meretricious allurement, and expecting an unfeigned love and gratitude

G 3

from her, whose smiles, like the butterfly
in summer, are only for the sunshine of
prosperity, and who looks forward to
the hour of adversity as the season of her
harvest! on that she seizes, and faithful
only to her interest, remorselessly aban-
dons the deluded victim on whom she
has entailed destruction.

Some time did the wretched Angelo
continue thus tottering as it were on the
verge of madness, yet struggling to be
reasonable; now wildly his thoughts
dwelt on Felix, his boy so fondly yet
so injuriously loved. Why had the
monster robbed him of his son, his dearest treasure? Confused, bewildered, as he
was, the suggestion was obvious. She
had made Felix the companion of her
flight, to evade the probability of pursuit; for with that vile artifice peculiar
to such as her, justly and cunningly

had she calculated, that however Angelo, aroused from his infatuation by her conduct, might determine to pursue her with justice, when he reflected that by so doing he must implicate his son, who must of necessity have been privy to the transaction, of which too she could adduce proof, he would abstain altogether from the attempt, anxious rather, however deep a sufferer he might have been, to give as little publicity as possible to the event; besides, he might hope by his forbearance towards her, to induce her to remand voluntarily the youth to him; whereas if he listened only to his revenge, she might not only secrete him for ever, but through him bring dishonour upon his name.

Suddenly Angelo started up from the supineness of despair; he remembered the obligations under which he existed,

and the necessity there was for his seeing Ellesmere that day. It was requisite he should impart to him the whole
of what had happened. With this idea
pressing on his mind, he hastily rushed from the house, but scarcely had he
gained the street than it was displaced
by another, which preserved the ascendancy; his first purpose was forgotten,
the image of the unfortunate Gabrielle
stood before him. Should Ellesmere, as
he was certainly entitled to do, have
waved courtesy, and promptly insisted
upon his right, she might at this moment be even destitute of a home.

Something like a sensation of horror
and remorse shot through his heart;
quick as lightning he directed his steps
towards the spot where she had continued
to linger, and arriving at the house,
with impatient violence assailed the door.

The instant it was opened, he flew past
the servant without an inquiry, and
bounding up the well known long deserted stair-case, sought unannounced the
apartment where Gabrielle usually sat.
She was not there, and he heard the
voice of the servant behind him, who informed him she was in her chamber;
thither he hastily proceeded, and bursting open the door, with wild disordered
look he stood before her.

Gabrielle, pale, emaciated, the image
of settled hopeless melancholy, lay ex-
tended upon a couch, almost too feeble
to move. At the sight of Angelo, so
long estranged from her eyes, and with
air and countenance that spoke some dire
ill, her weakened nerves were nearly
overpowered, a hectic blush of terror
and agitation flushed her hollow cheek;
not that she dreaded for herself an accu-
mulation of sorrow, of insult, or of out-

rage, for that was impossible, but she apprehended, she knew not what, and made an attempt to rise from her recumbent posture.

" Stay, stay," cried Angelo with a frenzied look, laying his hand upon her shoulder, " where would you go ? remain—remain, while yet you may."

" What!" cried the enfeebled Gabrielle, with a wild indignant look, while the tears rushed to her eyes,—" do you come to drive me hence ? Well, well, be it so, I am ready."

" I !—no, no ; but do you not know ? have you not seen Ellesmere ? this house is no longer mine."

" What mean you, Angelo ? or is this but an unworthy subterfuge to drive me hence ? Say—say openly—since it is your

6

will, I shall endeavour to gain strength,
—to *die elsewhere!*"

She rose, and leaning on the back of
the couch, like a pale spectre she stood
immoveable.

" Hear me! hear me, Gabrielle!"
cried Angelo ; and in the effort he made
to explain to her the truth, reason a little recovered her empire, " I have no
longer a house, nor you a home ; I am
become a beggar! you are so likewise!
This house, together with all I once possessed, last night became forfeit, and now
appertains to Ellesmere! Say then, have
you no pity for me, Gabrielle! can you
not feel?—Pity, did I say! ah, what
would it avail to a wretch like me, ruined, ruined, past redemption !" He sank
into a chair beside him, devoid of energy, and his senses again began to wan-
der.

Gabrielle became sensible of renovated strength, her firm elastic mind rose beneath oppression, with towering dignity; her faintly throbbing heart beat quicker, her languid pulse with accelerated motion; she was no longer feeble; with steady step she approached the nerveless Angelo, and laying her burning hand upon his arm, she said, "Tell me, Angelo, why in this moment have you thought of me? what have you done with Milborough? where is my son?"

"Why question me thus?" returned Angelo without raising his eyes from the ground, "but if you would know—where one is, there is the other likewise; learn moreover, and triumph—both have plundered me of all, and fled!"

Gabrielle spoke not; she raised her eyes, and lifted her fair hands to

Heaven, while the expression of her
fine countenance was, "God! thou
hast punished him enough; now is it for
me to sooth!" The loss of her child
conveyed an acute pang to her heart;
but the youth loved her not, and, all excellent, all amiable as she was, it was
not in nature for this reflection to be
wholly without effect. Angelo she beheld before her, in a state such as
implored oblivion of his errors; her
noble soul forgave that unconquerable
yet unjustifiable pride imbued in his
very nature, which, guilty as he must
feel himself, had not yet permitted
him to acknowledge his culpability
and sue for pardon at her feet; she
knew well his was a mind which required to be softened, rather than re-
proached into submission.

In the moment of adversity, he had

thought of her ; she was now all he possessed, and cruelly as he had outraged
her, he did justice to the magnanimity
of her mind and feelings. He had appeared before her a wretch weighed
down with crime and misfortune. He
might have yielded to a sense of shame,
and shunned her still ; but no, he had
humbled himself in her sight, by per-
mitting her to behold him thus punished, his conduct to herself avenged, and
had beseeched the pity of her whom
most he had injured.

These noble sentiments, these liberal
constructions, too liberal indeed towards
Angelo, whose weakness in the hour of
adversity, requiring the aid of firm and
energetic friendship, had had equal, if
not superior share in precipitating him
into her presence, awakened her heart
in his favour; and with the benignity of

a pitying angel she bent over him in compassion; consolation appeared to her to have become a duty, and in a sweet soothing voice she said,—" Angelo, arouse yourself, despair is impious; since your situation is such as you have described, let us consider only what remains to be done."

Angelo raised his lurid eyes, and fixed them upon Gabrielle; he beheld a countenance which resembled that of a sorrowing Madona, his heart was acutely touched : " And is it from *you* then, oh, ill-fated daughter of Montmorency !" he cried, " is it from you that first I hear the voice of consolation ? Oh, Gabrielle ! injured Gabrielle," he added hastily, " unless you would annihilate me at once, unless you would drive me to distraction, speak to me in another voice ! look on me with other eyes ! let your words

be daggers to my heart, and let your
glances be stern !"

"No, Angelo," replied Gabrielle, "at
this moment I can cherish against you
no feeling of bitterness. I am myself
a wretch meriting severest punishment,
my crimes exceed yours, and I hail misfortune as salutary chastisement, as a
proof that God has not wholly abandoned me, but would purify me for future
life, of which otherwise I should be too
unworthy ! If I grieve, Angelo,—if I
grieve, it is—that *you* should be the instrument of my punishment." Again
her pale face, her humid eyes were raised
to Heaven, and she seemed wrapt in the
fervour of her divine conceptions.

" Oh, spare me ! spare me, heavenly
being!" cried Angelo, glancing upon her
countenance, and hastily withdrawing his

conscious eyes ; " sink me not thus low,
but be merciful as you are above me !
Deign only to reproach me," he added in
a voice of bitter anguish, and bursting
into tears.

Gabrielle was recalled to earth; she
gazed upon her first love, upon the destroyer of her youth, upon the murderer
of her father, upon him who had blighted
his honourable hopes and her fair prospects—but she beheld only his tears of
agony—his wild dishevelled form !—she
forgave her injuries, and pressed his
burning head to her bosom.

Angelo sprang from his attitude of
despair to throw himself at her feet; he
embraced her knees, and kissed them with
frantic ardour, and raising his eyes to
her countenance, he cried, " Gabrielle, I
have betrayed, destroyed, and brought

your fair youth to destruction !—I have now become a wretch in misery as well as crime, beggared in every present and future hope ! Dare I then say it—it is only now I feel that fully I appreciate your exalted virtue ! it is only now, when such appreciation is but mockery to you, that it breaks upon my benighted soul, as the sun first sheds his dazzling rays upon the sight of him who has been for long in dreary blindness ! Here then solemnly I swear to Heaven, that I will dedicate to you the residue of my worthless existence. Gabrielle, look down upon me, now sunk into most abject misery ; I pledge myself in the sight of the God whom through you I have offended, to make you mine at his holy altar, should you even yet deign to accept me. I pray that he may visit me in all the thunders of his wrath, if ever more I deceive, abandon, or betray you."

" Rise, Angelo," cried Gabrielle in a mournfully solemn voice; "I accept your penitence, and would rather become yours at this moment, than in the height of your prosperity. But hear me, I am now childless, I have no dear interests superior to my own that require my consideration; above all I feel that though I should to-morrow become your wife, Heaven would not grant me long to enjoy a title that once would have sounded so sweetly in my ears!—I feel,—yes, I feel, that the death of my father will be, by a just Providence, avenged upon me!—I too am dying of a broken heart."

Angelo uttered a loud cry; his breast became filled with remorse, and penitence dawned upon his soul.

"Angelo!" said Gabrielle, in that tone of voice which is firm from the long accus-

tomed conviction of having nothing to
hope, " Angelo, be composed; since you
are once again returned to me, I shall not
yet die."

Angelo could not restrain his tears; he
sobbed, but Gabrielle could no longer
weep ; she made no effort to check the
tears of Angelo, for she conceived that
they preserved him from despair.

In the midst of this scene, the door
opened, and a servant announced the
name of Ellesmere; on Angelo it operated
like a thunder-clap, but Gabrielle bade
that he should be instantly admitted.

He entered with that gay and smiling
air usually worn by beings of the world,
who never by any chance attempt to anticipate even a moment of the future, en-
joying and thinking only of the present.

Gabrielle arose at his entrance, and involuntarily awed by the dignified grace of
her appearance, he bowed profoundly to
her, and advanced to Angelo, whom
he seized familiarly by the arm. " D'Albini," he cried, shaking him, " I am
sorry to see you thus crest-fallen ; I was
in hopes you knew me better than to com-
pare me to a vulgar creditor, I came only
now for the very purpose of observing
that I had no desire to *incommode* you.
But this house is extremely elegant,"
glancing on Gabrielle, "tastefully arranged, the pictures all from Italy, I
suppose,—ah ! I recognise the vivid
landscapes of Claude Lorrain !—the
masterly pencil of Correggio !—the brilliant colouring of Domenichino !—the
——"

"Sir," cried Gabrielle, interrupting
him, indignant at his loquacity, and the ap-

parent want of feeling displayed by Ellesmere, " the Count D'Albini is indis-
posed ; I have only to observe therefore
for him, in return for your polite attention, that this house and all that appears to
meet your approbation, will be at your
disposal by the evening."

" Oh, by no means," cried the man of
the world, still carelessly looking round
upon the pictures," oh, by no means ; nothing on earth would tempt me to inconvenience one of the softer sex, and particularly so fair a creature as yourself,"
bowing significantly.

" Sir," replied Gabrielle, turning aside
with dignity from his bold expressive
stare, " our arrangements are made ; by
this evening the house will be yours,
wholly yours,—will you for the present
permit it to be ours ?"

Ellesmere was what is termed a polished gentleman; he perfectly understood the hint of Gabrielle; and he had wit enough to perceive that idle compliments and presumptuous admiration might offend, but could not flatter her; bowing respectfully therefore, he moved towards the door, and as he opened it, he said, " D'Albini, we remain *friends,* I hope, in spite of *what has happened!*—Ah, willingly would I give all Fortune's favours," directing his eyes towards Gabrielle, " to be even now situated as you are."

Angelo endeavoured to command his voice, his pride came to his aid, and he replied, " Undoubtedly we remain friends, why not ?"

" Give me then your hand," cried Ellesmere, " in token of *amity.*"

With a sick smile, Angelo stretched
forth his hand, and the *friend* who had
rendered him a beggar, shook it as cordially as though he had been asking him
to dinner, bade him adieu with precisely
the same smile as he would have worn
to congratulate him on some good fortune, and would have felt as much interest
in the one, as he now felt regret at the other.

No sooner had Ellesmere departed,
than Gabrielle, with that prompt energy
which had ever marked her youthful
character, determined to employ the few
hours that remained till evening, in the
service of him who now possessed on earth
no friend but herself. For him she forgot
anguish long endured, whose baleful effects were for ever remediless, feebleness,
pain, indisposition, and this with only the
most desolate prospects before her, as
the reward for her highest exertion. She
persevered nevertheless, and with an

alacrity no way inferior to what his best
conduct might have claimed, adopted
such measures as she conceived best calculated for a speedy and prudential
arrangement.

From Angelo she now enquired more
particularly of an affair that had been as
yet but vaguely related, when it clearly
appeared to her that in saying he had
lost *all*, he had not exaggerated. Under
these circumstances it was only to sub-
mit with patience to what was unavoid-
able ; and while Angelo, plunged anew
into despair, by the detail of the ruinous transaction in which he had been engaged, remained incapable of action,
Gabrielle, a powerful instance of the
superiority of mind over matter, was
busily employing herself, feeble as she
was in body, in hastening the means of
final settlement, and departure from an

abode, which no longer considering their's, her pride revolted at remaining in.

Since the desertion of Angelo, she had retained only a couple of domestics in her own service ; these she found herself empowered to discharge to their satisfaction, and without their having a wish to remain where gloomy desolation had spread her pinions and prodigality no longer reigned. Her next consideration was to seek some shelter for the night ; it was impossible immediately to procure a situation, such as might suit with their present circumstances; she therefore determined to postpone this attempt till the morrow, and to avail themselves for the present of some temporary accommodation, since to remain where they were an hour beyond the appointed time was too repugnant to her feelings.

Thus, ere the arrival of evening, her vigorous management had arranged every necessary step, and they were enabled to take their departure from an abode which she at least could not view with aught of tender regret, from a recollection of the happy hours she had of late passed within its walls.

CHAPTER XXII.

WE now behold Angelo ruined, and unnoticed by his worldly friends, pillaged
and deserted by an abandoned mistress,
forsaken even by the child he loved, forgotten and shunned in his adversity by
all, save Gabrielle, by all save her whom
in his prosperity he had insulted, injured, and betrayed. She, and she alone,
was his firm sheet anchor in the storm;
his friend, his comforter, she accompanied him to a wretched abode, far, far
different indeed to those he had been accustomed to, an abode, such as would
have excited the contempt of ephemeral

friends, and which none would have entered who loved him not for himself
alone.

Gabrielle entered it, and smiled like
his guardian angel upon the desolate
walls; her smile was a ray of light
through his bosom, it revealed at once
comfort and despair, for it showed him
to himself unworthy of the bliss of calling such a creature his !

Yet in justice to the superior soul of
Gabrielle be it said, that all benignant
as she was, the compassion which she
showed towards Angelo was no longer
in any degree the effect of an idola-
trous love, neither could former duties
longer influence her, but it sprang from
a native and transcendent generosity ;
tender, forbearing and patient as she was,
she possessed a proud mind.

The primary source of her endurance in unparalleled suffering, was not in a mean, selfish, or ignoble passion, which crouched most abject beneath ill treatment, and which no indignities, no cruelty could alter ; not in such source did it originate, but in her duty to her children ; to bear and forbear, for *them,* she deemed not disgrace, but glorious martyrdom ! Fatal and unforeseen events had exonerated her from this sacred and painful duty, fraught throughout with bitterness and severest trial.

Firm and unshrinking she had bared her bosom to the darts levelled against it ; now she beheld him who had loaded her with remorse and anguish, beheld him distressed, agonized, humbled to the dust. It was not surely in the most abject nature still to love ! it could belong only to the most noble still to pity ! Such was Ga-

brielle's, she could cherish neither hate
nor revenge against him she had loved
once, neither could she still love
when her firm mind had received
conviction that the object was at heart
unworthy—but this precluded not pity,
and she felt it a duty incumbent on her to
perform from that, all that the profoundest and most invincible love could have
dictated. Exalted was the soul of Gabrielle, and beautiful her religion, which
taught her charity towards every one's
errors but her own.

Thus then the unhappy Angelo received from her unwearied attention;
she sought as much as possible to detach
his mind from dwelling on his situation,
and exerted herself to cheer and to soothe
him by such reasoning as was suggested
by the divine influence of fervent piety,
that looks not with a vain sorrow upon

the afflictions of this life, but extracts
from them the sacred hope of future
better existence, for which *sorrow* best
purifies the soul !

All was however vain: Angelo possessed not the towering mind of his comforter, he could not rise superior to the
influence of situation, he felt himself a
wretch within and without, surrounding
circumstances filled him with dismay,
and his conscience loaded him with reproach.

Nature by degrees became overpowered, he sunk into an alarming malady, and
incapable of opposing by energy or reason that useless regret and ceaseless repining which aggravated his disorder,
he was compelled to resort to his bed,
from whence never more he expected
to arise. Mean time Gabrielle, who la-

boured under a malady far more dangerous than that of Angelo, the malady
of the *heart*, who had been for long supported by her energies alone, now found
it necessary doubly to exert herself, and
to become the nurse and attendant of Angelo, as she was his only stay and hope.

It was requisite however to call in
medical aid, and this, together with the
additional expences incurred by his
illness, began to shew the alarming probability that such calls might ensue as
she would be unprepared to answer.

During the desertion of Angelo her
expenditure, never prodigal, had been
considerably abridged; it was owing to
this circumstance that she had been hitherto enabled to compass the difficulties
that had occurred, and to assist Angelo
when he no longer possessed resources

for himself. Her rational and anticipat-
ing mind, had not failed to suggest to
her, that in order to preserve themselves
from future dreadful embarrassment, it
would be necessary that some plan
should be resorted to, to prolong their
present trifling means of subsistence.

The whole treasure they mutually
possessed were the jewels of Gabrielle,
and a small sum in specie. These of
themselves could not long suffice, and
hence the necessity conceived by Gabrielle of concerting some plan for future
support, ere the present means should be
entirely exhausted. The illness of Angelo, however, deranged and frustrated
her intentions; already she had found it
requisite to part with a few of her most
inconsiderable ornaments; and learning
from the physician she had employed
for him, that he conceived him in a state

which would render it prudent to call
in other advice, she perceived there
would exist an inevitable occasion for
parting immediately with the most valuable ones.

The recovery of Angelo being a primary object, she determined that every
consideration should yield to it, whether
of calculating prudence or otherwise.
As soon therefore as the physician who,
after visiting him declared his opinion
to Gabrielle, had departed, she returned
into the chamber of Angelo, and approached his bedside.

With that eager anxiety, which in
sickness is naturally manifested towards
one whom experience has proved to be
the only earthly being interested in their
welfare, Angelo, soon as he saw her,
stretched forth his feverish hands, and

in a faint voice exclaimed, " Oh, Gabrielle, tell me, am I to live or die ?"

" Live, assuredly," she replied with
a celestial smile, and tenderly taking his
hand. The indisposition of Angelo was
chiefly occasioned by the indulgence of
a useless and consuming grief, which
he had neither fortitude nor energy to
repel, rather than any real bodily ailment.
It was a strong affection of the nervous
system, accompanied by deep depression
of spirits and extreme irritability, which
rendered his malady more alarming than
dangerous.

Frequently trifles would overcome
him so much that he would burst into
tears; thus the feebleness of his mind increased his physical debility, and rendered him incapable of the smallest
exertion.

Now that he beheld Gabrielle standing beside him, and looking upon him
with that tender benignant countenance,
he was suddenly struck with the remem-
brance of the evils he had brought upon
her, and could not avoid contrasting his
conduct with the generosity and magnanimity of her's toward him ; the impression was too strong for his disorga-
nized feelings, tears rushed to his
eyes, and incapable of restraining his
emotion, he sobbed aloud. Gabrielle,
infinitely affected, sat beside him, and
endeavoured her utmost to sooth : by
degrees she succeeded, and when she observed him calm, she said, " Angelo, it
will be requisite that for a short time I
should leave you ; will you promise me
that you will endeavour to sleep ? I shall
then have the satisfaction of knowing
that you will not want any thing during
my absence."

" What, are *you* going to desert me too at last?" cried he, in a mournful voice.

" But I will return immediately; will you not trust me, Angelo?"

" And if I should die in your absence, who will care for the wretched Angelo? who will visit his cold corpse?—no one, no. Ah! who would ever have thought such could have been my fate?" At this he shed bitter though silent tears, while Gabrielle almost wept to perceive such lamentable imbecility of mind; but fearing to increase by joining in this vain depression, she subdued her emotion, and cried, " Oh, my dear Angelo, you must conquer these melancholy ideas; believe me it is a weakness, wholly unworthy you. If you desire that I should not quit you at present, most certainly I will

6

not; yet if for a few moments you could permit, I should rather, for sooner or later I must;—I will procure you an attendant during my absence."

"An attendant!" exclaimed Angelo, "what! would you leave me to the mercy of hired wretches?—Oh, my God! let me die at once, if such is to be my lot."

Gabrielle, who had arisen, now patiently resumed her seat beside him; she thought it useless and improper to irritate him by further argument, and secretly determined that if, as she hoped, he should fall into a slumber, she would seize that opportunity of escaping to dispose of her jewels, and return home with all the speed in her power. Angelo remained silent for a considerable time; Gabrielle flattered herself he

was asleep, and to ascertain, she made
a gentle movement to rise. Immediately Angelo with a violent start drew
the curtains aside; his face was pale as
death, over which his dark hair hang-
ing dishevelled, gave him an air of wildness.

"Gabrielle! for God's sake do not
leave me yet," he cried; "I think I
shall be better in a little time, and able
to bear your absence; but will you not
inform me where you are so desirous of
going ?"

From the air of alarm visible in his
countenance, the idea now first struck
Gabrielle that he really apprehended she
intended if possible to escape from him,
and desert him. Feeling for the horror
with which such an idea must impress
his weakened mind, and anxious that

for a moment even he should not continue
to indulge it, she decided rather to acknowledge to him the real object of her
mission abroad, though under other circumstances she would infinitely have
preferred the concealment of it, lest it
should give to his heart a pang she could
spare him. Looking at him with a smile
therefore, she said, " Since you are so
desirous of knowing my motive, I will
not disguise it from you, and then I
hope you will have no further hesitation
at parting with me for a few moments. I have some jewels, which are
altogether useless to me, in our present
state—my object is to dispose of them,
as—as I have occasion for money."

Angelo with a sudden spring raised
his weak frame in the bed; he fixed his
eyes upon Gabrielle with a wild stare,
his features were convulsed, and in a

faltering voice he said, " What—what
jewels do you mean?"

" I will shew them to you," answered Gabrielle, wishing to divert his emotion, which she attributed solely to the
sad necessity she had inferred of parting with her jewels, and rising, she approached a small trunk in the room,
from which she took those she had intended to dispose of, and brought them
to Angelo. The instant he cast his
eyes upon them he uttered a groan of
anguish, his lips quivered, he clasped
his hands together, and sinking back, he
faintly murmured " They are false !—
they are false !"

" False !" cried Gabrielle, who beheld with horror, if Angelo spoke reason, her best hopes destroyed ; " False,
said you?"

" Oh! yes, yes," groaned the agonis-
ed Angelo, " *I robbed* you of yours, and
placed those in their stead! I——"
Overcome by his terrible feelings, he
made a frenzied attempt to spring from
the bed, and cast himself upon the floor;
the feeble strength of Gabrielle opposed
itself to his, she with difficulty retained
him in bed, and in a state of insensibility his beating head fell heavy upon the
pillow.

Alone, unaided, Gabrielle applied
herself to his restoration; by degrees he
recovered from apparent death, but it
was only to vent in delirium his weakened powers; he raved aloud—he inflicted blows upon his shattered frame ;
and the overpowered Gabrielle, finding
it longer impossible to cope with him,
beheld herself under the painful necessity of calling in other aid; and abso-

lutely exhausted, Angelo at length fell
into a sleep, deep and profound as the
sleep of the tomb.

Gabrielle seized that opportunity of
leaving the room for a moment, and
without quitting the house, found she
could procure for him an attendant, one
of those persons who, in offering their
services for the sick, have no other idea
than of the emolument to be thus deriv-
ed, and whose sources of livelihood are
in the misfortunes, sickness, and distress
of others. This being, Gabrielle was
however glad upon any terms to hire,
and every step she took convinced her
more and more of the necessity there existed of obtaining some speedy means of
compassing her encreased expences.

As the mind of Angelo could not at
this juncture be considered in a state

of sanity, the introduction of a stranger
into his apartment could excite no unpleasant feelings.

With a heavy heart, Gabrielle then
proceeded to gather together such
other ornaments as she still possessed,
and made a selection from them of those
she considered most valuable, and capable of supplying present exigencies.
Reluctantly then resigning to the care
of the attendant the still sleeping Angelo, she hastily departed to dispose of
them the best she could.

Unfortunately for her, however, she
discovered that the worst possible period
of attempting to obtain money, is precisely that in which it is most needed.
Those to whom she applied, easily perceived, that though she wished to obtain for her jewels the utmost that she

could, in default of obtaining what
she wished, she must of necessity take
what she could procure; this was
enough, the extremity so dreadful for
her, was their harvest, and that advantage was unfeelingly reaped from her
distress, which perhaps had not otherwise been thought of; for one half of
the world lives and flourishes by the
misfortunes or follies of the other half.
Thus she was compelled to accept a
fourth part only of what she had flattered herself with easily obtaining, and
returned to her chearless home with
a heavier heart than she had left it, and
her mind filled with gloomiest forebod-
ings of the future.

At length the physicians who had
been called in, either in compassion for
the evident embarrassment of her situation, or under apprehension that their

attendance and advice must ultimately
remain unpaid, informed her that they
had ascertained the malady of Angelo
to arise solely from an undue irritation
of the nerves, that it was more of the
mind than of the body, consequently
irremediable by the art of medicine, and
that they therefore could be of no further service.

Such being the decision of the physicians, Gabrielle was once more determined to undertake alone the charge
and restoration of Angelo ; she dismissed,
therefore, the attendant she had tempo-
rarily hired, (who in daily expecta-
tion of his death had anticipated from
the anguish of Gabrielle, and her con-
sequent indifference to worldly matters,
no inconsiderable booty, of which she was
thus disappointed,) and enacted herself
at once into nurse, physician, and at-

tendant, and by her judicious management and tender care had soon the happiness of beholding Angelo in a gradual
state of amendment.

He recovered perfectly his reason, and
his body being so much debilitated by
sickness, he was no longer subject to
paroxysms of delirium. In a short
time he became enabled to quit his bed
for several hours in the course of the
day, and ultimately to forsake it altogether. But this change was not produced by magic, it cost the patient perse-
vering Gabrielle infinite pain, distress
of mind, and the privation of almost
every comfort in existence; her care
was unremitting, indefatigable, she
scarcely slept by night, or rested during
the day, and intent on procuring for
Angelo every nourishment that might
restore his strength, she almost forgot to

take any for herself, and remembered to
do so only, when her failing powers informed her, that in order to support him,
it was necessary she should support herself.

But the time was now arrived when
the sufferings of Gabrielle were to exceed
all she had hitherto experienced. Till
this period, though want had gleamed in
perspective upon them, and well she
knew that it must approach, if some
means of keeping it at a distance were
not devised, still want in perspective,
and immediate want, are widely different,
for the one is only imagined, while the
other is felt ; one excites apprehension,
and the other despair.

Gabrielle had now parted with every
article of value she possessed ; next she
had parted with all which the most rigid

necessity did not compel her to retain,
and now having nothing more left which
might be bartered for subsistence, she
with a shudder beheld that the gaunt
fiend was rapidly approaching, and that
if exertion were not instantly made to
elude its fell grasp, soon it would over-
power them.

Yet it was not for herself that Gabrielle felt or shuddered; to her, death
would have been but a transition from
perpetual misery to eternal peace, she
would have hailed it with joy, embraced it with eagerness; but for the
sufferings of another, she had not fortitude to die! all her anxiety was for
Angelo, all her indifference for herself.

As Angelo was however now so much
restored both in mind and body, he would

permit her to leave him sometimes, and even with patience endure her absence. Thus when Gabrielle beheld that their means were so rapidly decreasing, and that ere long they must completely cease, she one day quitted him with the resolution of not returning till she had obtained some mean of certain subsistence, and to shrink from nothing, not in itself dishonourable, that might enable her yet a little longer to support with the forsaken Angelo the burthen of existence.

With this purpose therefore settled in her mind, though undecided as to the mode of pursuing it, she wandered along the populous streets, musing as she went, unobserved, or if observed, unnoticed; for her air bespoke unhappiness, and her attire poverty, appearances not calculated certainly to attract the pleasure-seeking eyes of the world. Who, indeed, need apprehend officious observation that under *such* circumstances wanders forth !

Passing a print shop, accidentally she raised her eyes; she beheld in the window a various assortment of drawings, so placed as to strike the beholder to the best advantage ; involuntarily she stopped, for she had an exquisite taste in drawing, which the departed Montmorency had delighted to cherish and improve, and an idea had flashed across her mind that induced her hastily to approach the window : she inspected the prints, and a modest sense of her own superior powers in designing and co·louring such subjects as were before her, consisting chiefly of flowers, caused her pale cheek to mantle with a conscious blush, and yielding to the sudden im-

pulse which actuated her, timidly she
entered the shop.

The cold money-getting face of the
man within damped in an instant her
rising hopes and deranged her ideas.
She was aroused however by the com-
plaisant inquiry of what she desired,
and forcing herself by an effort to overcome the emotion of shame, so naturally
felt by a noble mind when for the first
time it beholds itself in the novel situation of dependance, she faltered out an
intimation that she would be happy to
be employed in that branch of his mer-
chandise which consisted in flower painting.   She stopped, and the unusual
throbbing of her heart informed her,
that for the first time she had asked *a
favour!*

From the obsequious, kind and smil-

ing countenance of the man who sells his
goods, and *receives* for them money, this
person's changed suddenly to the proud,
consequential, and imposing countenance of the man who purchases, and
gives money; for there is a wide difference with beings of this description, between the act of receiving even the merest
trifle, and that of giving it; the first
still leaves them in the rank of the person obliged, the latter places them in
the important and unusual light of having conferred a favour.

Of these opposite positions the person whom Gabrielle addressed was perfectly sensible; he therefore in a careless
and familiar tone replied that he had no
objection to oblige her if she was in *distress*, though he had already more ap-
plications than he could attend to, and
more hands than he knew how to

employ; he concluded by observing that the difficulties of the times were great, and that he could not undertake to promise any great consideration for the very best style of painting.

All this the proud daughter of Montmorency bore, for she felt that her purpose was good: the difficulty of compassing that which required to be done, always strung her energies anew; she acceded therefore to the hard terms and mercenary stipulations of the shopkeeper, with an anguished smile, and returned home with employment sufficient for several days.

Gabrielle was again in a novel situation, that of labouring for a livelihood; still she acquitted herself, as hitherto she had done, to admiration. "Oh! spirit of my father!" would she ejacu-

14

late, " could'st thou look down from thy
bright abode, thou would'st not disapprove; *this* would not have vexed thy
mortal pride to heart-breaking, for in this
there is *no dishonour !*"

As she reflected that had she at this
juncture been reduced to absolute
want without the means of procuring
even the morrow's meal, Providence
would thus have assisted her, and ward-
ed the horrors of such a day; she felt
her heart glow with gratitude to the
throne of beneficence, and with a pleasure such as for long she had not experienced.

Thus are we ever the creatures of immediate predicament ; the circumstance
which at one time to anticipate might
have overwhelmed with despair, proves in
its occurrence at another a source of re-

joicing ; events take their hue from the
moment, and are only good or bad ac-
cording to their comparative relations.
Who could have imagined that the
talents of Gabrielle, cultivated beneath the
tender care and elegant instructions of
her father, would ever have availed her as
a mean of livelihood, or that she should
consider herself fortunate in procuring
with difficulty the opportunity of rendering them such ? Yet thus it was,
though only a few years back she would
have viewed the bare possibility of present certainty with horror almost stag-
gering belief.

Reaching home, Gabrielle applied
with alacrity to her task, and, such is
the divine effect of energy, felt even her
mind lightened by such application,
though confessedly for bread, and di-
verted from the contemplation of sur-

rounding ills. But Angelo was incapable of emulating her, incapable even of attempting to do so; he could only gaze with wonder and admiration, without being animated by a portion of her heavenly fire; so true it is that great minds only can bear adversity. Gabrielle, though thus she laboured and exerted herself more for the benefit of the unhappy imbecile Angelo than for herself, endeavoured, with her genuine delicacy, to disguise that it was absolutely for support that she did so; she worked with cheerfulness, and sought rather to impress upon his mind that it was chiefly for amusement she thus occupied herself.

She dreaded he should feel that he depended upon her for subsistence, and her superior soul shrank from weighing him down with such a sense of obligation, and from a gratitude that, far from pleasing, would have distressed and shocked her.

But Angelo could not be for ever thus deceived; he beheld the incessant toil of this noble but unfortunate being; he beheld too that it was for him she toiled; the sense of his own unworthiness pressed heavy on his heart, and while it filled him with a profound melancholy, still further incapacitated him from what he would have considered a fruitless exertion to cope with or join his efforts to hers.

Often would he gaze upon the downcast, pale, and fading countenance, to which the gay flower she was painting and decking with all the animation of nature, formed, as it bloomed beneath her hand, a garish contrast. Often

would he consider that while calling into
artificial life by the magic of her pencil
the frailest productions of nature, she
was herself withering fast into real decay, perishing while she bade them
bloom. Often then would he burst involuntarily into a passion of tears, throw
himself at her feet, seize her wan
hands, kiss them, and regard her with
an anguish that defied the power of
words.

In the mean time, however, the most
active exertions could not balance her
expences : as Angelo appeared still de-
clining, she could not resist the desire of
procuring for him every delicacy that
she conceived likely to tempt or allure
his sickly appetite, and though she lived
upon the coarsest fare, and would not
allow herself even a sufficiency of that,
still daily she found her means becoming

more and more inadequate, for though a miser, she was such to herself alone.

One evening that she was as usual busily employed, she felt a sudden weakness coming over her, her eyes grew dim, her head giddy, her trembling fingers relaxed their hold of the pencil, and unable to conquer the overpowering sensation, she sunk back in her chair.

Angelo, terrified, flew to her assistance; she made an effort, and with a languid smile entreated him not to be alarmed; scarce had she uttered the words, ere her heavy head, in which a thousand bells seemed jingling, dropped upon his shoulder, and her senses fled.

Now was Angelo compelled to exert himself; he took her in his arms and placed her on the bed, chafed her sunken

temples and cold hands, shed over her
torrents of tears, and in bitter anguish
accused himself of having murdered the
most angelic being upon earth; but had
he known the true cause of Gabrielle's
indisposition, what then would have been
his sensations, what his self-reproaches?
The truth was, that intent as usual upon
Angelo, and regardless of herself, she had
expended almost the whole of the trifling
sum she had in the morning obtained, in
the purchase of a delicacy of which she
knew Angelo to be extremely fond; it was
however expensive as it was rare, and
Gabrielle determined not to partake of
it, that the gratification might be prolonged to Angelo.

Yet how evade his earnest persuasions?
The idea suggested itself of affecting that
she had taken refreshment while abroad,
and was incapable of accepting more,

though at the same time nothing had
been further from her intentions, as such
she would have deemed wanton expenditure, after having already gone far beyond what her slender means might au-
thorize ; and she promised herself that
she should find no inconvenience in dispensing with an occasional meal, as long
as by so doing she could procure some
indulgences for Angelo.

But Gabrielle, neither apprehending,
nor respecting the delicacy of her nature,
acted more in conformity to its spirit
than to its strength. In considering only
the first, she over rated the last, and from
dispensing in the commencement with
one meal less a day, and sensible of no
immediate injury, she next dispensed
with two, and ultimately often with
any. This was one of those days on
which she had not tasted food, and had

been without from an early hour on the day preceding. She had walked, exerted herself, added by various efforts to her exhaustion, and had ventured without allowing herself the smallest refreshment, to resume, as soon as other cares had been completed, her occupation. Nature however was no longer capable of enduring such cruel imposition, and sunk beneath the extraordinary efforts she required from it.

When by degrees she recovered from her swoon, she became sensible of the cause that had induced it, and yielded to the entreaties of Angelo that she would take a little of the wine she had procured for him, which was one of those luxuries she still persisted in obtaining for him, and ever as resolutely refused to partake of. For the present however she consented to relax in a slight degree

the severity of her laws against herself,
and, as Angelo supported her in his arms,
accepted from his hand a small portion
of the wine, which considerably revived
her, and she became enabled to rise from
the bed, but still so much enfeebled
as to be under the necessity of abstaining
more reluctantly from her employment,
though she was sufficiently imprudent to
hazard the attempt.

CHAPTER XXIII.

From this period Gabrielle grew daily worse, yet determined to persevere till the power of doing so should utterly forsake her. She disregarded the strong and faithful warnings of nature, which on every exertion, however trifling, appeared on the point of being overpowered, and still pressed and goaded it beyond its capability of endurance. She felt a rapid internal waste, her strength failing, and every indubitable symptom of hastening decay.

The origin of her malady was certain-

ly in the mind; now its baleful effects
had communicated to her body in an
alarming degree; the least movement
fatigued her, to bend over her employment caused a pain at her chest, amount-
ing to suffocation, to walk was an effort
carcely endurable, and her only moments
of comparative ease were when for a
few hours she allowed herself in a recumbent posture to seek the benefit of
repose.

She now became so extremely feeble,
and was so frequently obliged to inter-
mit her occupation, that she clearly perceived she must speedily relinquish it
altogether.   On this subject however
she was spared consideration; for having
one morning, with infinite pain, dragged
her weary limbs as far as the residence
of her employer, for the purpose of con-
veying home the fruits of her labour;

the unfeeling being, upon receiving
them from her, looked coldly in her languid countenance, and carelessly observed that she seemed going into a consumption, and too ill to work.

The unfortunate Gabrielle, shocked at
this cruel remark, shrank back, yet timidly replied, " that such light work
could not possibly injure any one;" ill,
dying as she was, she thought of the feeble Angelo, and still was anxious to preserve for him the means of procuring a
slender subsistence.

" That's no concern of mine," replied
the man, in answer to her observation, " all I know is, you work too slow
for me, and I can't pay you above half
price any longer."

Gabrielle answered not, for though

she despised the brutality of the man,
she easily perceived that remonstrance
must be lost upon him, and that he was
one of those vilely selfish beings who
have no other idea than that of trafflick-
ing with distress, and think all fair that
may be reaped from the urgent necessi-
ties of the unfortunate : she did not
therefore notice his insinuation, for well
she knew the pain and labour which it
cost her to compleat what she did for
the miserable consideration which she
received; to have performed it for any
thing beneath that, much less half, as
this being had intimated, would, she felt,
have been absolutely useless. Stretching forth her fair hand therefore, she
accepted the wretched pittance which
was her due, and without deigning to
utter a syllable, left the shop.

Now was her situation indeed dread-

ful ; she saw that want must speedily
overtake them, that nothing could delay
its rapid strides ; she entered their sad
abode with tottering steps, and a heavy
heart, almost incapable of further exertion, had she even retained her employment.

Angelo was dismayed at her appearance ; she looked the chill image of
breathing death, or like some shadowy
phantom bearing the false semblance of
life and reality.

In tender accents he enquired the
cause of her seeming anguish ; for though
her pallid aspect was familiar to him,
there was an expression of distress in it
at present, such as, owing to her perpetual exertions to appear cheerful in his
presence, he had not for long so evident-
ly perceived.

Her fortitude half succumbing at the sad prospect she now anticipated for Angelo, she looked in his face with the wish to smile, but burst into tears.

"Ah, tell me, beloved Gabrielle, what has happened!" exclaimed Angelo.

" Nothing, nothing, poor Angelo; nothing has happened, but the time is at length arrived—we must starve together!"

Angelo, who had scarcely during this period of distress experienced aught which could be termed privation, and whose mind therefore could not be like Gabrielle's, familiarised to the idea of want, remained for a moment stupified with horror at her words, and the manner in which she had uttered them.

"Wretch that I am!" at length he exclaimed, striking his forehead with his hand, "wretch that I am, and monster! it is I, who have caused all this! Oh! Gabrielle, Gabrielle, on my head rest your sufferings, on my head will be your death."

"Not so, Angelo," faintly cried Gabrielle, "accuse not yourself, neither give way to despair; consider, dear friend, situated as we are, existence is rather painful than pleasing; if you then can with calmness bring your mind to the idea of its surrender, wherefore should we grieve, since passing from this state cannot fail to be a transition to a better? But for you, long, long had I anticipated that æra with hope, as now I view it without regret."

But Angelo possessing not the fortitude of Gabrielle, could not reason like, nor think with her; life, however bitter, was preferable in his estimation to death, the idea of which, as usually to weak minds it is, was terrible to him, viewed with repugnance and dismay. He cast himself in despair upon the ground, and could offer no consolation to her who had so long veiled from his eyes; though fully revealed to her own, the picture of horror now displayed before them. Oppressed by the strong power of imagination, already he fancied the hand of death upon him, and again were the waning powers of the hapless Gabrielle exerted to restore him to firmness and better thoughts.

The first transports of despair over, urged by the pious counsels and elevated reasonings of the half-sainted Gabrielle, Angelo, gradually animated

by a slight portion of her divine enthusiasm, acquired the power to contemplate
without shrinking the scene before him.
He beheld indeed that the best hope
now was, death bringing a speedy termination of their remediless woes ; it was
death in its apprehension, rather than the
settled thought of death, which appalled
him ; it was its slow approach which he
dreaded—the pang of seeing it advance,
that he wished to be spared, and he prayed
in his heart that it might overtake him
suddenly, and without warning, or that
in unconscious slumber, his trembling
soul might pass into eternity.

The day at length dawned upon the
wretched pair, when not only their
means of procuring further subsistence
were totally at an end, but when they
had not even sustenance to support
them through it—not even a single

slender meal. This was indeed a day of horror for Angelo—to Gabrielle, of pious resignation, firm hope, and blissful anticipation of a future, better state.

Till now Angelo had resembled the mariner in the storm, who to the last moment indulges hope, nor amid the crashing wreck resigns it, till dismayed he sees rushing towards him the mountainous surge which must envelop him in its fathomless bosom. So till this day, vainly, weakly and unreasonably, had Angelo indulged the fond hope of some unforeseen event, some blest occurrence to turn the tide of fate, and preserve him from the catastrophe, so dreadful and incredible to his mind, of perishing from want.

Yet this fatal day had already dawned, and no symptoms of an approaching de-

livery had appeared—it advanced unvarying—evening arrived—they gazed
at each other in silence—night followed,
and as the darkness spread around them,
Angelo started from the fixed attitude
of despair in which he had been gazing
on Gabrielle, and clasping his hands
together, exclaimed, "Now indeed have
I lost all hope, the crisis of our fate
rapidly approaches, God enable us to
meet it with courage ;" then in a deep
gloomy voice he pursued, " Gabrielle,
canst thou bear my head upon thy knee?
I could sleep—wilt thou then pray, that
from the arms of sleep, gently I may pass
into those of death !"

" Come then, my dear friend," cried
Gabrielle, " so be it ; for myself, I will
not sleep—my crimes have been great at
the bar of heaven ; I would employ my
last moments in endeavouring to prepare

my guilty soul for its examination, and praying of the Almighty to judge it with mercy."

Angelo threw himself at her feet, he laid his head upon her lap, and covered his eyes with her hand, as if desirous to shut out for ever all earthly objects, and be spared the *pang* of death.

Soon as he wished, deep sleep overpowered him. The apartment was in gloomy darkness—yet the inspired soul of Gabrielle saw light—her thoughts ascended to eternity, and revelled in the infinity of space. In the heaven of heavens she fancied she beheld her father, that he looked down smiling upon her, and with outstretched arms, and in a voice which seemed to her rapt ears as the music of the spheres, said, " Come, my Gabrielle, all is forgiven."

In visions like these did she pass the
night, sleep visited not her eyes, neither
did she wish it.   Morning dawned, Angelo started suddenly from his slumber,
and springing up, exclaimed in a wild
voice, " Oh, my God ! do I then still
live !"

" Be not impatient, my friend," said
Gabrielle ;   " but if thou hast strength,
bear me to the bed, that I may die
there, for of myself I have not power to
move."

Angelo, who was somewhat refreshed
by sleep, bore the enfeebled Gabrielle
in his arms to the bed, and seated himself beside her.   This day the sun shone
upon them, but its splendour was mockery ; Gabrielle gazed not on it through
humility, for she wished not that its
cheering beams should exhilarate her

soul, or recall her to earthly pleasure, while Angelo closed *his* eyes upon the brilliant visitant in the bitterness of an impatient despair.

Hour after hour rolled on; the dusk of evening again advanced, a sense of pain from long abstinence began to be acutely felt; their sufferings by this most terrible of deaths were necessarily protracted, and gradually increased, while their termination was contemplated, by the one with an invincible fortitude, by the other with sensations of an indescribable horror that amounted almost to madness!

The light was now such that they could merely distinguish each other. Gabrielle in a faint voice murmured to Angelo, to raise her head from the pillow. Trembling with anguish and alarm,

he obeyed, conceiving from the tone of
her voice that her last moments were approaching. He supported her in his
arms, she rested her head upon his
shoulder, and gazed on him, though
without speaking, with a grateful placid
smile. She laid her spread hand upon
her heart, her eyes of celestial blue
were raised upwards with an animated
expression, her countenance was that of
a saint inspired with a holy fervour, while
her soul seemed gently passing like a
breath from earth to heaven !

Angelo looked upon her with the
wild aspect of moody terrible despair,
on perceiving that he must still survive,
yet with an anxious wish that her fleet-
ing breath might be delayed till his
might mingle with it, and their souls
together pass the threshold of mortal
life; for he dreaded the thought of dy-

ing as it were unprotected in his last
moments, so tremblingly did he hang on
Gabrielle, even in death.

While thus they remained in each
other's arms, a slight noise was heard at
their door. Gabrielle, whose thoughts
had already parted from earth, wished not that they should be recalled to it;
she desired to die ; and to return to life
and to the world, would have been a
painful effort ; she heeded not therefore the noise, either by look or movement.

Mean time it was repeated, but with
increased violence. Angelo started involuntarily; it continued still louder,
for their door had been secured, that no
one might intrude upon or witness their
anguish and distress. The attention of
Gabrielle was dragged again to earth,

K 5

she made a faint movement, Angelo laid
her head gently upon the pillow, and
fast as his debilitated limbs would allow, approached the door, opened it, and
in a voice almost inarticulate from passion struggling with weakness, he cried,
" Who dare intrude here! and interrupt
our last moments!" at the same time
staring wildly upon the intruder, and
holding the door in his hand, as if unwilling he should enter.

" D'Albini!" cried a voice that recalled itself to the mind of Angelo, " I
perceive you know me not; I have, however, letters and papers of consequence
for you, which I could deliver into your
hands alone: with the utmost difficulty,
after having been several days in search
of you, I have been so fortunate as to
trace you; and if I judge aright, you will
find in the packet I bring something to

reconcile you to my apparently unwel-
come intrusion."

Angelo now perfectly recognised the
voice of an old associate, but his travelled
heart shrunk from contact with him,
and in faltering accents he replied, his
native pride still operating. "This is
no place for you, it is the chamber of
misery, of death !—I will dispense with
your entrance, you can have no papers,
no letters that *now* concern me."

"Pardon me," returned Fitzarden,
"and allow me a word only, to convince
you to the contrary. Ellesmere is no more,
he expired by a wound received in a
duel from his most *intimate friend*, who
had attempted to seduce his mistress: no
sooner was he given to understand that he
could not survive, than he sent for me, and
reverting to his unfortunate transaction
with yourself, the whole of which he

had before related to me, he confessed that in that awful moment he felt the bitterest remorse, from the reflection of having, as he feared, completely ruined you, since you had suddenly vanished, no one knew whither ; and that he could not die easy, unless he made you restitution of the whole of what he had obtained from you on that memorable night, and at every former period. "Promise me,.Fitzarden," he added, "that you will not neglect my dying request, that you will not rest till you have discovered his retreat,. and re-instated him in the full possession of his own." I faithfully promised ; he lived to see the requisite instrument executed, which was to confirm you in the possession of your right, and then expired in comparative tranquillity—though deeply deploring his manifold errors, yet in the hope that he had retrieved at least the effects of one most baleful." Fitzarden concluded ;

Angelo endeavoured to speak, hope had dawned upon his soul, and with it had returned, more strongly than ever, the desire of life.

The attempt, however, that he had made to speak, from the confusion of ideas that pressed upon his mind, and his extreme debility, overpowered him. He staggered towards the bed, where the silent Gabrielle still lay ; he essayed to express himself to her, but could not ; the words evaporated in a hollow murmur, and he sunk exhausted on the bed. Fitzarden, now considerably alarmed, called aloud for lights and some assistance.

Angelo was presently restored, though appearing in a state of the utmost debility ; but for the unhappy Gabrielle, her last hour seemed to have arrived, and it was considered almost a forlorn hope

to summon the immediate aid of a physician.

Without making enquiry, the situation of his former gay companion was
sufficiently evident to Fitzarden; he
clearly perceived that he was reduced to
the most abject distress, and as he cast
his eyes around the cold desolate apartment, he could not avoid contrasting
it in his mind with the sumptuous dwell-
ings in which formerly he had been accustomed to behold him. The view of
the dreadful change produced by a fatal indiscretion, struck a salutary terror
to the heart of the young man, and he
started to reflect that his own habits
were at this period such precisely as
D'Albini's had long been: thus reverting to self, and what might be his own
fate, he felt his commiseration in-

crease for the unhappy beings before him.

A physician now arrived, and was conducted instantly to Gabrielle; he felt her pulse, looked in her death-like countenance, on which the finger of want had imprinted traces deep as those of sorrow, and pronounced with an unusual delicacy and sincerity, that her malady was the result of intense exhaustion, and that nourishment, not medicine, was alone capable of restoring her.

At this declaration, however compassionately veiled, that the tender and angelic Gabrielle was expiring from want, Angelo, unable to restrain his acute emotion, burst into tears. Such was the anguish of his feelings, that but for immediate assistance he would have sunk

into a state worse far than that from
which he had just been recovered.

Despair and 'eternal repining had
made on his countenance a havoc almost equal to that which want and
hidden anguish had made in that of Gabrielle; and again as Fitzarden pressed
him to take some wine, he gazed upon
his sunken cheeks, and hollow eyes, and
could not avoid remembering the gay
hours when, glowing in the bloom of
health and careless vivacity, they had
pledged each other in repeated goblets,
not, as now, to restore exhausted nature,
but to sink it rather in enfeebling sen-
suality, or, plunging into the vice of
prodigal excess, to fit themselves for
pursuits that sober reason could not
have tolerated.

Some exhilarating cordial having

been administered to Gabrielle, she once
more opened on the light her faintly
beaming eyes.—Angelo supported her
in his trembling arms; while Fitzarden,
in whose soul the scene before him
awakened feelings which he was unconscious of possessing, and whose mind
was impressed with the most delicate
respect for Gabrielle, joined his entreaties to those of Angelo, and earnestly
besought her to take some nourishment.

Gabrielle found herself compelled to
yield; the cup of existence was again
presented to her lips, she wished not to
taste of it, for her sad mind foreboded
that as heretofore the sweets that it
might contain, would bear no proportion to the bitter with which they would
be mingled; yet to repel life was equal
to the crime of seeking death; she re-

membered that she was the creature of
her Creator, and as her piety had given
her the resignation to die, it now inspired her with the fortitude to live.

She recovered by degrees; with her
Angelo recovered likewise, for he saw
that for this time he should be spared
the remorse of beholding her die for
him. His was not a mind to anticipate distant events, neither to dive deeply into remote origins, or causes : the
simple position of not having to accuse
himself at this juncture of the death of
her who had sacrificed so much for him,
who had famished that he might feast—
to be spared a reflection so bitter, so
accusing, was of itself sufficient to exhilarate his soul, while the idea, then
shining forth in added lustre, of his fair
future prospects, conveyed a feeling of
renovated bliss. Fitzarden would not

leave them till he beheld them in a
state widely different from that in which
he had found them; Angelo, ever easily
depressed, now animated to a pitch of
extravagance, while a feeling of pleasure at *his* joy, chastened by her stronger
reason, shone through the lovely mind of
Gabrielle, as the mild light of the soul,
or like a tempered sun-beam diffusing
around a soft and tender brilliancy.
Fitzarden promised to return on the following day, but previous to his visiting
them, to arrange for their reception an
abode somewhat different to that which
they at present occupied.

" But was not this good enough to
die in !" observed Gabrielle to Fitzarden, as he rose to depart.

" I know not that," answered Fitzarden, who involuntarily gazed on her

with admiration; " for such a being as
you it was not even good enough to die
in; yet indeed," added he, " virtues like
yours are of themselves independent,
requiring neither living pomp nor mau-
soleum !"

" Who talks of death!" cried Angelo,
with a laugh,—" it must be life, beloved Gabrielle, long and happy life,
for both you and me !"

The feelings of Gabrielle told her a
less flattering tale, but she faintly smiled in compliment to the wild hopes of
the sanguine Angelo.

CHAPTER XXIV.

A FEW days now beheld them reinstated in all their former comforts, such at least as depended upon ease and affluence alone : but while other subsequent sufferings had diminished in the mind of Angelo the feeling of deep sorrow for the loss of a son, and then again by an unexpected deliverance from those sufferings, made him almost forget the evil in the good, the heart of the sensible Gabrielle fondly yearned after her children, in anxious conjecture of their fate, and in the eager desire to behold them ere she died ; for sadly she

foreboded that if this period did not soon
arrive, speedily must she resign the lingering hope.

And well and truly did she forebode;
that tender and susceptible soul had received a cureless wound, which time
might aggravate indeed, but which it
was powerless to heal. Great and terrible, even from early youth, had been
her sufferings, almost unintermitting;
one misfortune had been succeeded by
another, and each more dreadful than
the last. Those blows which render
some hearts callous from their frequency, had lacerated her's beyond recovery;
yet it was not that she wanted firmness
to repel, but she had likewise sensibility
acutely to feel.

Such, such on a virtuous, delicate,
and sensible mind, are the consequences

of early error, deeply, unceasingly, yet unavailingly deplored.

Now that Angelo was restored to the rank he had formerly held in society, he determined to renew to Gabrielle the offer of his hand; for his vices were in consequence of the weakness of his heart, and not of its depravity—of the insufficiency of his reason to direct him right, and not of his desire to do ill. He reverted therefore with complacency to the idea of making Gabrielle his wife, and with that pleasure which never fails to accompany in a mind not utterly depraved the desire of retrieving in some degree the faults that have been committed, he felt, with becoming emotion, how little was this late and insufficient compliment calculated to recompense in the thousandth part, the conduct she had pursued towards him.

He seized therefore the earliest opportunity of fulfilling his intention, and
in justice to him be it said, with a faltering and confusion resulting from the
consciousness of how much earlier he
should have made the tender of that
name and title, she had ever equally as
now deserved.

"When I was young and foolish,
Gabrielle," said he, "I knew not your
worth; I outraged, injured, and insulted
you : when I became beggared in fortune as in happiness, I felt a wretch so
wholly unworthy of you, that to have
then pressed upon you the offer of my
hand, would have merited that you
should reject it with contempt; but now
that I am no longer in adversity, though
bettered by the lessons it has taught me,
and capable from the point of view in
which it has revealed your excellencies,

of appreciating, though not yet equal to your merit, the heavenly treasure I possess in you; now if you will suffer me by repentance and future care to expiate in a slight degree my past errors towards you, then, beloved Gabrielle, will you give me but one more proof of the superiority of your nature, even in that difficult task, the forgiveness and oblivion of injury.

Gabrielle gave her hand to Angelo in token of acquiescence : confused ideas pressed upon her mind, she wished not to damp his animation, nor the hope which sparkled in his eyes, fondly bent upon her, by giving them utterance; therefore looking with kindness on him, she remained silent, while she admitted without pain to her mind the conviction that long she should not live to possess by name, what in a su-

perior degree she had ever been in character.

Angelo was permitted to fix an early day
for the ceremony of rendering Gabrielle
his wife ; he desired to invite the whole of
his friends (so esteemed) resident in Eng-
land, to witness what he termed the cele-
bration of his day of triumph ; but from
this public display the pride and delicacy of Gabrielle shrunk repugnant, knowing too well that it would be considered
by others the day of *her* triumph ! It
was enough for her to receive in secret
the tardy avowal of her merits; the morti-
fication of having been so long unappre-
ciated, or deemed unworthy, and of accepting at length what had been ever due to
her, was by her deemed no proud triumph;
to be exhibited before idle witnesses,
who could neither feel nor understand,
none either, but the contrary. In secret

had been her sufferings, her injuries, and indignities; of the atonement which it was proposed to make for them she had her own sentiments, and she determined that secret too should be her acceptance of it.

The day now drew nigh on which the marriage was fixed to take place. Gabrielle, still languid, feeble, and becoming daily more exhausted, reclined upon a couch from morning until night, and on the arrival of the day, she was so ill as to be incapable of the least exertion.

Angelo with his usual impatience was wild at the idea of being under the necessity of postponing the ceremony, which Gabrielle no sooner perceived than in order to tranquillize him, she declared her determination that no indisposition

on her part should retard it.—It took
place accordingly; she received his
vows and gave him hers in return; and
Angelo, as he embraced, and hailed her
by the name of wife, experienced a feli-
city purer and more extatic than ever
had been afforded him by the highest
gratification of meretricious passion.

Such is the power of virtue over the
heart, that even a long course of vice
will not render us wholly invulnerable to
its divine influence; yet if indeed there
be a human being so far sunk in depravity, as to prove an exception to thi
remark, lamentable indeed must be his
state.

But the performance of a sacred cere-
mony had no power to call back to Gabrielle her departed health; it had no
more power over her weakened body

than over her towering mind her ; fearful malady continued to increase, and she
appeared but as a fair anatomy, the shadow of her former self. Angelo, who
perceived that of all his worldly friend-
ships Gabrielle had alone remained
by him in the hour of adversity, viewed
her at length as she had always merited to be viewed, and could not contemplate the possibility of losing her,
without feelings little short of distraction.

Now as the prospect of her danger
increased, his anguish and his fears increased likewise ; he ransacked the king-
dom for advice, he collected around
him a host of doctors : all proved vain ;
and in despair of the power of medicine,
he yielded with the eagerness of a last
hope to the counsel which directed him
to convey her from the dense atmosphere

of the town to the salubrious coast of Devon.

The patient uncomplaining Gabrielle, who took without a murmur the vain medicines which the terrified solicitude of Angelo pressed upon her, who listened with a placid and resigned smile to all that was proposed, who yielded with the softness of an angel to every scheme suggested for her amusement, or the renovation of her health, acceded without a word of opposition, and without a thought of hope, to the present entreaty of Angelo, that she would at least consent to try the effect of a purer air.

As if he had obtained a certainty of prolonging her life, of restoring her from wasting sickness to bloomy health, he seized her acquiescence on the instant, as fearful she should retract, and by the

eager impatience which he evinced in
preparing for the journey, if he distressed and incommoded the enfeebled Gabrielle, he at the same time conveyed to
her mind the reflection that she was now
more than ever dear to him ; though why
she was so, she wished not to dissipate
the pleasing delusion by inquiring.

In the highest human mind, self-love
will a little operate ; true, the conviction
could not restore her drooping health,
but it spared her the pang of witnessing
in the last stages of her existence a root-
ed heart-breaking indifference to her
fate.

With Angelo, to decide and to act
was the same thing ; he immediately left
London, and by easy stages arrived in
Devonshire, there hiring a beautiful
cottage which commanded an uninter-

rupted view of the coast. In the exhilaration inspired by novelty and change of scene, Angelo, transferring his vivacity to the idea of Gabrielle, endeavoured to believe that it arose from beholding in her languid countenance confirmation of his hopes that her residence on this spot would be crowned with success; expressing himself to her with his wonted animation, he exclaimed, gently seizing her in his arms, " Come, my love, come, recover your bloom ! you must—and the brilliancy of those eyes; smile upon me, and let me see that already you feel yourself growing better !'

As if in obedience to his wish the pale countenance of Gabrielle became suffused with a faint hectic blush, and unwilling to damp the animation of Angelo, she said, " I do, Angelo—I do feel growing better;" she smiled too, but her

smile was hopeless, and the momentary
fire which sparkled in her eyes, was in
the blest anticipation that she would be
better, not in this world but in a future
state.

Several weeks she lingered, at the
earnest wish of Angelo, in this lovely
abode. It was the close of spring, and if
hope of health could be conveyed to
the sick soul bending to the tomb,
this was the season to inspire it; or if
life could be breathed into the cold
form of death, this too was the season
in which the miracle would have seemed less ; but amidst all this, amidst its
mild verdure and budding beauty, the
heart of Gabrielle was incapable of being
elated, it was still calm, still patient
and resigned, for she felt that no *second*
spring could it ever be her lot to behold!

One evening when for the time of year
it was uncommonly, but not oppres-
sively warm, Angelo prevailed on her to
sit without the door of their cottage,
and inhale the refreshing breezes from
the sea; she as usual acquiesced, he led
her forth, and debility compelled her
immediately to sit upon the rustic bench
which had been placed for her accommodation. She leaned back, and Angelo,
with his arm round her waist, tenderly
supported her of whom now he felt
almost the full value.

Nothing could be more beautiful than
the prospect before them; it was nature,
not in her most fantastic or magnificent
attire, but in her simple, lovely and most
interesting garb! she was not as a fierce
and sovereign mistress decked in her
robes of state, and awing by her frowns,
but as a gentle maid, wooing and irresis-

tibly winning admiration by her dim-
pled smiles. Gradually sloping hills,
dales, and blooming valleys, charmed
without confusing the senses, pleased
without fatiguing the eye; before them
the green expanded bosom of the sea
seemed swelling in soft acclivity, and as
if respectful to the sun beams glittering
upon it, (making it a sheet of liquid ra-
diance,) only gently smiled, and undu-
lated, sending to the shore at intervals its
low rushing waves, that in hollow murmurs seemed to speak their gratitude.

Gabrielle sat for a while silent, her
dim shining eyes fixed on the prospect
before her; mournful, yet not unpleasing
ideas crouded on her mind—she shed a
few tears, but they were not tears of anguish. " Angelo," cried she at length,
" regard the sky."

" I behold it, my love," answered Angelo.

" Do you see nothing remarkable in it?"

" Nothing!" Angelo replied, looking at her involuntarily with some surprise.

" Well then, regard stedfastly," pursued Gabrielle ; " do you remember the figure of my sainted father? look!" pointing with her finger, " it is *there* accurately delineated in the sky! see, there is his majestic form! the contour of his head, his perfect self! Ah, Angelo, he is in heaven, he is *behind* that cloud, and his blest image shines dimly through it, as through a thin veil! ah! now it fades! it fleets away! see, Angelo, it is disappearing altogether! Would that my soul could aspire on that parting sun beam, and reach him ere he goes—He came to call me hence! to warn me, I know it—I feel it in the new sensation that rushes through my frame! I am going to be regenerated!" She paused for a moment, then added in a voice, low yet firm, " Angelo! never more on this earth shall I behold the glory of the setting sun!"

" My beloved," cried Angelo turning pale, and half fearful that her senses were forsaking her, or that her language was ominous of approaching death, " my beloved, talk not thus, nor let so fair an evening inspire you with melancholy only—it should chear, it should exhilarate your spirits, for I am confident from the improvement I behold in your looks, that it has benefited you; never, never did you appear more beautiful in my eyes than at this moment!"

Nor was the latter observation of Angelo wholly void of foundation, on the livid white of her cheek, glowed but not blended with it, a crimson red, resembling the brightest hue of the damask rose-bud! the gaudy and deceitful livery in which fell consumption often decks its victims, misleading with the hope of health, when nearest to the tomb! The bright red tint which gave to her eyes a delusive brilliancy, causing them to shine like distant twinkling stars, added to the semblance of beauty, which Angelo had remarked; but Gabrielle, whose inward feelings taught her the vanity of looks, mournfully shook her head, and said, " Deceive not yourself, Angelo, nor cherish vain hopes; endeavour," she continued in a deep solemn voice, " endeavour while I have yet strength to touch upon a subject nearest to my heart, to listen to me with fortitude:—Promise me, when I am gone

that you will spare no pains to learn the
fate of our children!—promise me, that
for their sakes, you will form no other
tie, and that being free, and at liberty,
you will employ the time after *my death*,
in seeking to discover if still they live,
and *how!* Oh! Angelo, this is a mo-
mentous consideration; I cannot but
think that we, to whose unhappy errors
they owe that ever they were ushered
into life, *must* be responsible for their
fates at the bar of heaven! I wish not
to grieve, to torture you in my last moments," for the countenance of Angelo
bore evident symptoms of the acuteness
of his feelings, "but if I speak not now,
as I feel it my duty to do, never more
shall I possess the power!

"The only atonement which now we
can make for our crime, is to obviate as
much as possible its fatal consequences.

Think, Angelo !—Great God ! we have
two children, and at this moment as if
heaven were determined to punish us,
and show its wrath at the subversion of
a *moral duty*—at this moment we are
deprived of both! nay, in utter ignorance of their destination !—dreadful
reflection !—Yet if Heaven, more merciful than just, should wave in *our* favour
the great cause of *society* (for in the
grand scale of its wisdom, the few must
not be spared in their errors to the injury of the many) and not punish as we
merit, through us, those innocent victims—if you are allowed life, as I am
not, yet to retrieve the unhappy past—
then, I beseech you, give, give your whole
soul with ardour, with enthusiasm to the
task ! Ransack the universe for your
children, and snatch them from impend-
ing fate ! Oh ! thrice blest will you be,
should you be permitted success ! thrice

blest will you be, and happy will you
die, if laying your hand upon your heart,
and fixing your eyes on heaven, you can
say, "*God*, I thank thee, my *children* suffer not through *me* !—neither at thy tri-
bunal can they accuse me !"

The voice of Gabrielle, sweetly solemn, sunk in the heart of Angelo,
but it deprived him of hope, and he gazed upon her with tearful eyes. It was
getting dim twilight; to his inspired
fancy, she appeared as an embodied
spirit ! he dared not even take her hand,
such was the sacred awe of his feelings,
and though her words rived him with
anguish, he waited in hallowed silence
for what further her aspiring soul should
dictate to her lips !

She resumed: "You are silent, Angelo;
I perceive, and I bless heaven for it, that
you are impressed by my words ; it is all

I wish; I would not depress your soul,
I desire rather to imbue it with energy;
nor, if departed spirits are allowed to
look down on this earth, could mine,
oh, Angelo! be half so approving of
your grief, as in beholding you in active
prosecution of my *last* desire!"

"Oh, Gabrielle!" cried Angelo sinking on his knees before her, "beloved of
my soul, talk not thus, I implore you, of
your *last* desire! of quitting me at this
moment, when you are more dear to me,
more valued than at any former period
of my past life! Oh! no, I will not promise aught—I cannot—I shall be bereft
of energy if deprived of you! Live, live!
oh, Gabrielle! and to the remotest corner of the earth may you command me!
Inspired by the dear hope of rendering
you happy, I should acquire strength,
ardour for any thing! obstacles would

but increase my exertion, and if our children still lived upon the earth, to your eager arms would I assuredly bring them!"

As he concluded, Gabrielle sank down upon her knees beside him, and joining his hands together, held them in hers.

"Now swear!" she cried, "now promise, Angelo, that you will faithfully attend to what I have required of you! —*promise,* or in peace I cannot die!— till then my soul, reluctant to leave its tenement of clay, will struggle in agony for mortal life! and e'en when parting hence, will still be steeped in anguish, unsatisfied, and clogged with remorse at the bar of heaven!"

"Oh! great God!" cried Angelo, bursting into tears, "you rive my heart-

strings.   Look not thus, my beloved !—
Yes, I *swear,* I swear."

" God! I thank thee!" cried Gabrielle, extending her fair arms to heaven,
and looking upwards with a smile of en-
thusiastic gratitude; then kissing the
forehead of her husband, she added,
" Raise me, dear friend, and lead me into
the house."

Angelo obeyed, but rather carried
than led her light emaciated form into
the house; she retired early to bed, and
slept with composure during the night.

On the following morning Angelo
entered her chamber ; she was sitting up
in her bed, supported by pillows; the
un, through clustering vine and jessa-
mine, shone brightly into her apartment, and with singular pleasure was

she regarding alternately its chequered beams upon the floor, and the fair prospect without, while a variety of birds gaily singing and joining in concert their small melodious throats, seemed striving at once to inspire her with joy and hope, and to serenade the rising morn!

Poor Gabrielle was gazing with that melancholy anxious look that evinced her consciousness it was for the *last time* she did so; and this feeling, whether inspired by the anticipation of death, or absence, ever-gives an indescribable charm to the most trivial surrounding objects. Angelo approached her bedside, and tenderly enquired how she felt.

" Well!" replied she, " calm, easy, just as I *wish to feel!*" A pang struck the heart of Angelo at the peculiar expression of her countenance, as she uttered this; but endeavouring to conceal his feelings, he said in a gay tone, "Since you have awakened so early, Gabrielle, you may as well enjoy the fresh morning breeze."

"I would with pleasure," she answered, "but I feel too feeble; and perhaps if I could, it might be wrong—for it might give me a longing to inhale it again!"

"A longing that you might easily gratify, my love," interrupted Angelo.

"No, Angelo! I have seen the sun *rise*—I shall *never* see it rise again, nor shall I behold it *set!*" She reclined her head upon the pillow, and remained silent, while Angelo turned to the window to hide his gushing tears:—presently,

from her gentle and regular breathings,
he believed that she had fallen into a
slumber; he gently approached the bed,
and perceiving that her eyes were closed,
sat down beside her.

She slept for about an hour, but not
composedly; her countenance frequently
changed, her muscles now and then
worked with a tremulous motion, and a
cold dew broke out upon her forehead.

Suddenly she started and awoke, as in
trepidation and horror! she gazed with
a wild bewildered air around, seeming
anxious to collect her scattered thoughts,
and recover from her strange confusion!
Angelo, infinitely alarmed, took her hand;
at this she started anew, made an effort
to speak, and gazed on him with a look
of patient anguish on finding she could

not ! her fingers convulsively grasped
his, and now relaxed their hold—now a
thin film gathered over her eyes, and
now with a wild vacancy involuntarily
they opened wide! now the colour fled
from her lips, rushed back for a moment,
then forsook them altogether! Her
breathing became short and irregular,
and the terrified Angelo laying his
hand upon her heart, found its pulsa-
tions to tally with it.   He instantly
dispatched some attendants for the physician, who daily and vainly had visited her, and the moments passed in waiting for his arrival were past in anxious
trepidation by Angelo.

Gabrielle remained in the same state ;
she could not speak, but her fixed and
heavy eyes were turned on him with
an expression, such as convinced him
that she knew him well, and had even

something that she wished to say to
him.

The physician at length arrived; no
sooner did he behold her than, turning
to Angelo, he whispered, " I cannot
give you *hope!* her last moments are approaching." He drew near the bed-side
of Gabrielle, and raising her head he
poured into her mouth a few drops of a
restorative quality. Gabrielle faintly
struggled, an effort of nature aided the
effect of the cordial—she rivetted for a
few moments her closing eyes upon
Angelo, and made a movement with her
head, as if anxious to lay it on his bosom.

He took her in his arms, her head
fell heavy on his breast.—" Angelo !"
she faintly murmured—" a just God

visits——the death of my father upon
me——I——I too am dying——of a
broken heart!"

Angelo had not words, he looked on
her in anguish too big for speech; uttering a short convulsive sigh, she grasped his hand, and in quivering, irregular
accents hastily resumed,—" Remember
—our children—remember—your promise!" What more she sought to articu-
late in hollow murmurs died away, the
damps of death gathered on her brow!
cold and stiff became the hand which
Angelo, fevered with agony, still held
in his! the last breath flitted from her
livid lips, and her pure soul, now at liberty to seek a sphere more congenial
to it, ascended with it from earth to
heaven!

For many minutes after she had ceas-

ed to breathe, Angelo durst not admit
to his mind the terrible truth that she
was gone for ever! He continued gazing
on her cold body with a mingled sensation of agony, despair, and stupefac-
tion!—at length he turned away his
eyes, as if to convince himself that they
had deluded him only with a frightful
vision, and that when again he looked
upon her, he should behold her breathe!
but as he turned, he encountered the solemn looks of the physician, who, thinking that he read in the countenance of
Angelo something like an expression of
doubt, uttered the slow and dreadful
sentence,—" All is indeed over !"

" No, no! you dare not say it !"
wildly raved Angelo, clasping his hands
together,—no, no ! I am not so cursed !
—I have not killed the most angelic
being!—Speak! Speak, oh, Gabrielle !

say that you live!—that you *will* live!
God of mercy!" he continued, madly
glancing around, " she will not answer!
—oh! she is, she is indeed dead!!—
but I will not survive her—oh! no, by
heaven! not an instant!" and rushing toward the door, with intent to seek some
weapon of destruction, he was opposed
by those around, when in the wildest
fury he beat his breast, tore off his hair,
and as if determined on death, dashed
himself upon the floor, shrieking forth in
bitter cries the name of Gabrielle!
Then suddenly breaking from those who
held him, he sprang to the bed, fran-
ticly he embraced the inanimate form,
sacredly beautiful in death! he called
upon her in a frenzy of agony, till losing all command over his voice, it wandered into a latitude of horror scarcely
human! His senses failed him, and the
physician conceiving that, exhausted by

his violence, he would be longer unable
to resist, desired that he should be immediately conveyed to bed, and for that
purpose was he raised from the body of
Gabrielle.

At this movement his paroxysms returned, he struggled like a maniac, now
crying aloud that he would die beside
her, now piteously entreating that he
might be permitted! but nature could
endure no more, he became again overpowered, and sinking into insensibility,
was borne from the spot.

END OF VOL. III.

W. Flint, Printer, Old Bailey.

GOTHIC NOVELS

An Arno Press Collection

Series I

Dacre, Charlotte ("Rosa Matilda"). **Confessions of the Nun of St. Omer,** A Tale. 2 vols. 1805. New Introduction by Devendra P. Varma.

Godwin, William. **St. Leon:** A Tale of the Sixteenth Century. 1831. New Foreword by Devendra P. Varma. New Introduction by Juliet Beckett.

Lee, Sophia. **The Recess:** Or, A Tale of Other Times. 3 vols. 1783. New Foreword by J. M. S. Tompkins. New Introduction by Devendra P. Varma.

Lewis, M[atthew] G[regory], trans. **The Bravo of Venice,** A Romance. 1805. New Introduction by Devendra P. Varma.

Prest, Thomas Preskett. **Varney the Vampire.** 3 vols. 1847. New Foreword by Robert Bloch. New Introduction by Devendra P. Varma.

Radcliffe, Ann. **The Castles of Athlin and Dunbayne:** A Highland Story. 1821. New Foreword by Frederick Shroyer.

Radcliffe, Ann. **Gaston De Blondeville.** 2 vols. 1826. New Introduction by Devendra P. Varma.

Radcliffe, Ann. **A Sicilian Romance.** 1821. New Foreword by Howard Mumford Jones. New Introduction by Devendra P. Varma.

Radcliffe, Mary-Anne. **Manfroné:** Or The One-Handed Monk. 2 vols. 1828. New Foreword by Devendra P. Varma. New Introduction by Coral Ann Howells.

Sleath, Eleanor. **The Nocturnal Minstrel.** 1810. New Introduction by Devendra P. Varma.

Series II

Dacre, Charlotte ("Rosa Matilda"). **The Libertine.** 4 vols. 1807.
New Foreword by John Garrett. New Introduction by
Devendra P. Varma.

Dacre, Charlotte ("Rosa Matilda"). **The Passions.** 4 vols. 1811.
New Foreword by Sandra Knight-Roth. New Introduction
by Devendra P. Varma.

Dacre, Charlotte ("Rosa Matilda"). **Zofloya;** Or, The Moor:
A Romance of the Fifteenth Century. 3 vols. 1806. New
Foreword by G. Wilson Knight. New Introduction by
Devendra P. Varma.

Ireland, W[illiam] H[enry]. **The Abbess,** A Romance. 4 vols.
1799. New Foreword by Devendra P. Varma. New
Introduction by Benjamin Franklin Fisher IV.

[Leland, Thomas]. **Longsword,** Earl of Salisbury: An
Historical Romance. 2 vols. 1775. New Foreword by
Devendra P. Varma. New Introduction by Robert D. Hume.

[Maturin, Charles Robert]. **The Albigenses:** A Romance.
4 vols. 1824. New Foreword by James Gray. New
Introduction by Dale Kramer.

Maturin, Charles Robert ("Dennis Jasper Murphy"). **The Fatal
Revenge:** Or, The Family of Montorio. A Romance.
3 vols. 1807. New Foreword by Henry D. Hicks. New
Introduction by Maurice Lévy.

[Moore, George]. **Grasville Abbey:** A Romance. 3 vols. 1797.
New Foreword by Devendra P. Varma. New Introduction
by Robert D. Mayo.

Radcliffe, Ann. **The Romance of the Forest:** Interspersed With
Some Pieces of Poetry. 3 vols. 1827. New Foreword by
Frederick Garber. New Introduction by Devendra P.
Varma.

[Warner, Richard]. **Netley Abbey:** A Gothic Story. 2 vols.
1795. New Introduction by Devendra P. Varma.